bring bring!
Joe's

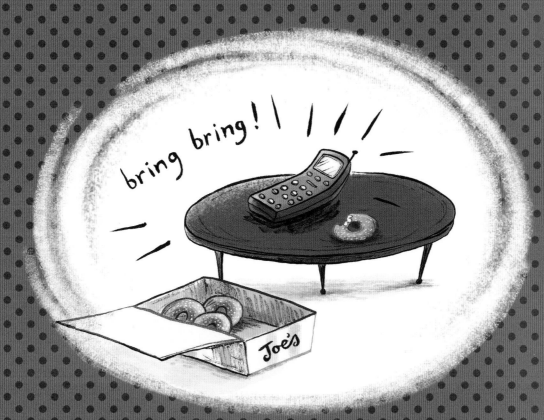

For Sarah, one of my two favourite nieces! – M.S.

For Lee, who solved the problem of how a worm
puts on a bandana xx – S.W.

BLOOMSBURY CHILDREN'S BOOKS
Bloomsbury Publishing Plc
50 Bedford Square, London, WC1B 3DP, UK

BLOOMSBURY, BLOOMSBURY CHILDREN'S BOOKS and the Diana logo are trademarks of Bloomsbury Publishing Plc

First published in Great Britain by Bloomsbury Publishing Plc

A catalogue record for this book is available from the British Library

ISBN 978 1 4088 9305 0 (HB)
ISBN 978 1 4088 9306 7 (PB)
ISBN 978 1 4088 9304 3 (eBook)

1 3 5 7 9 10 8 6 4 2

Printed and bound in China by Leo Paper Products, Heshan, Guangdong

All papers used by Bloomsbury Publishing Plc are natural, recyclable products from wood grown in well managed forests.
The manufacturing processes conform to the environmental regulations of the country of origin.

To find out more about our authors and books visit www.bloomsbury.com and sign up for our newsletters

The DON'T PANIC GANG!

Mark Sperring

Illustrated by Sarah Warburton

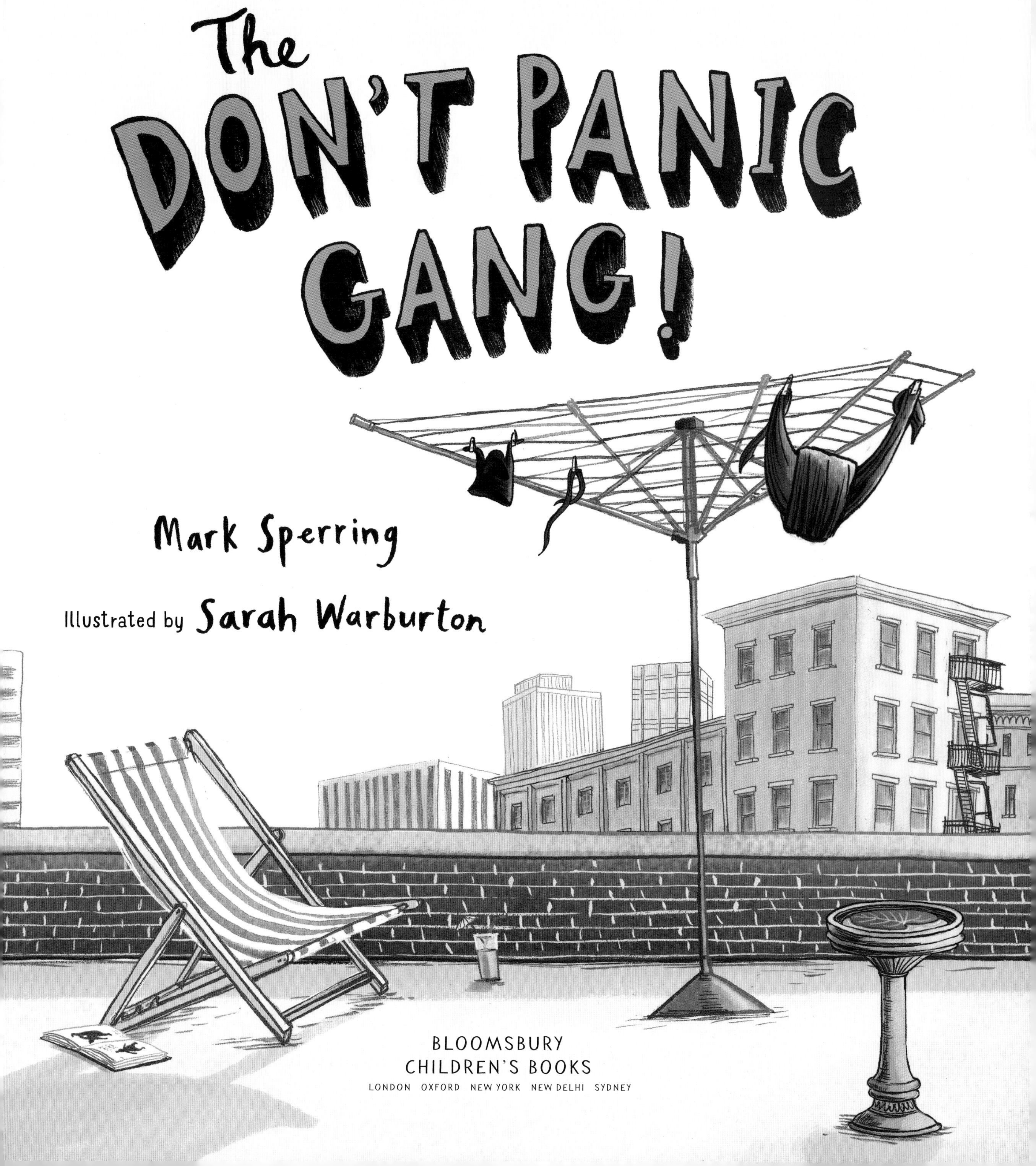

BLOOMSBURY
CHILDREN'S BOOKS
LONDON OXFORD NEW YORK NEW DELHI SYDNEY

In a big, BIG city, next to Joe's World-Famous Doughy Doughnuts, is the TOP-SECRET headquarters of . . .

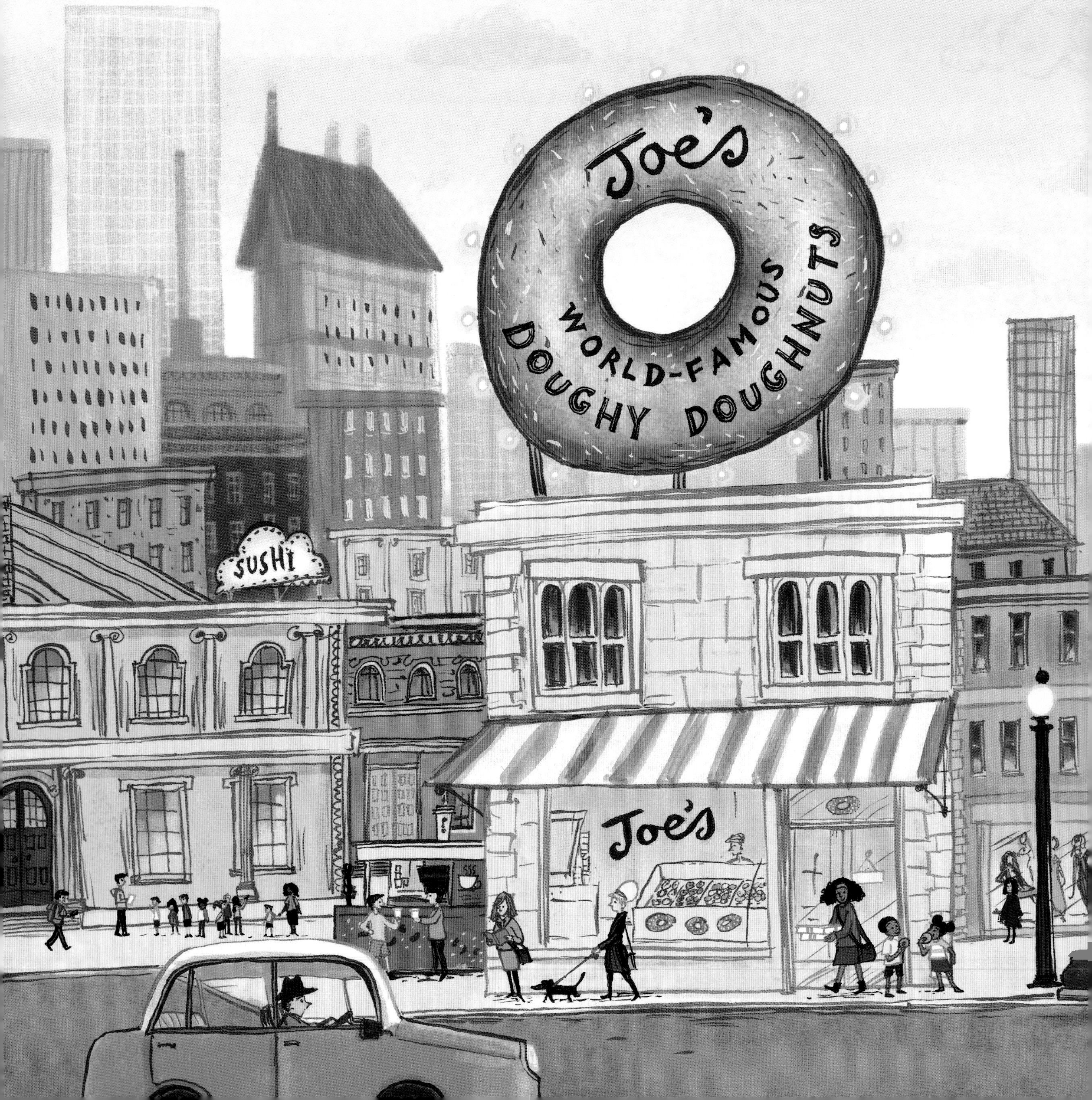

Joe's
WORLD-FAMOUS
DOUGHY DOUGHNUTS
SUSHI
Joe's

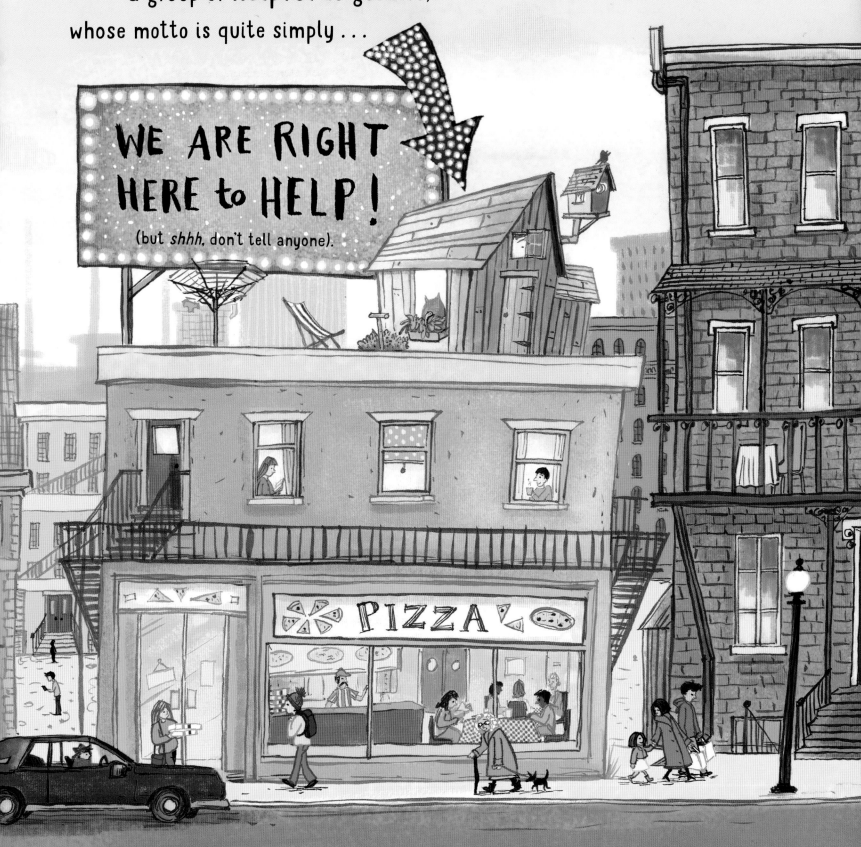

THE DON'T PANIC GANG,

a group of **helpful** do-gooders,

whose motto is quite simply . . .

WE ARE RIGHT
HERE to HELP!

(but *shhh*, don't tell anyone).

At first glance they are an ORDINARY-LOOKING bunch.

Just a doughnut-loving cat and a sweety tweety bird and a plain old window-box worm.

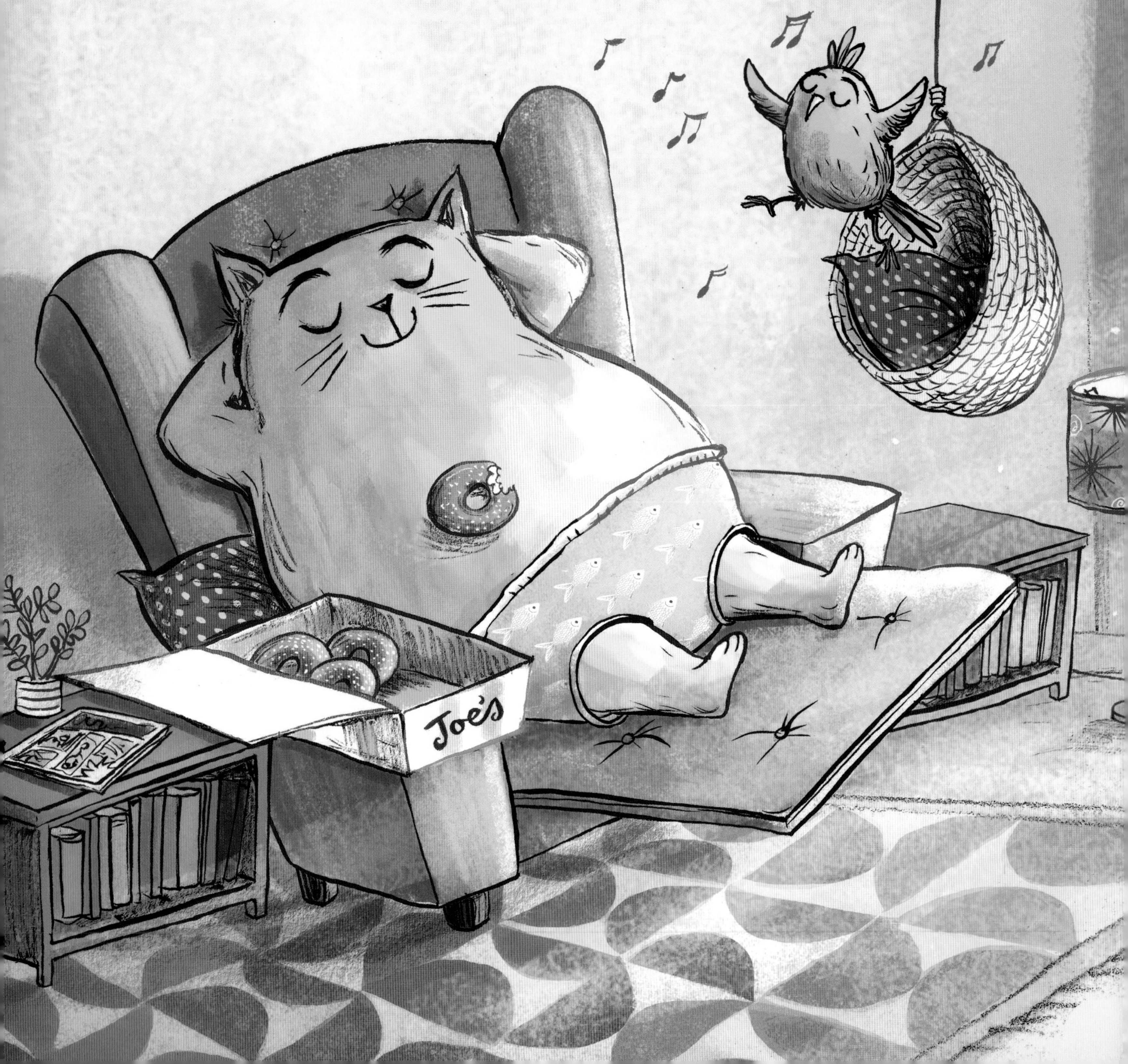
Joe's

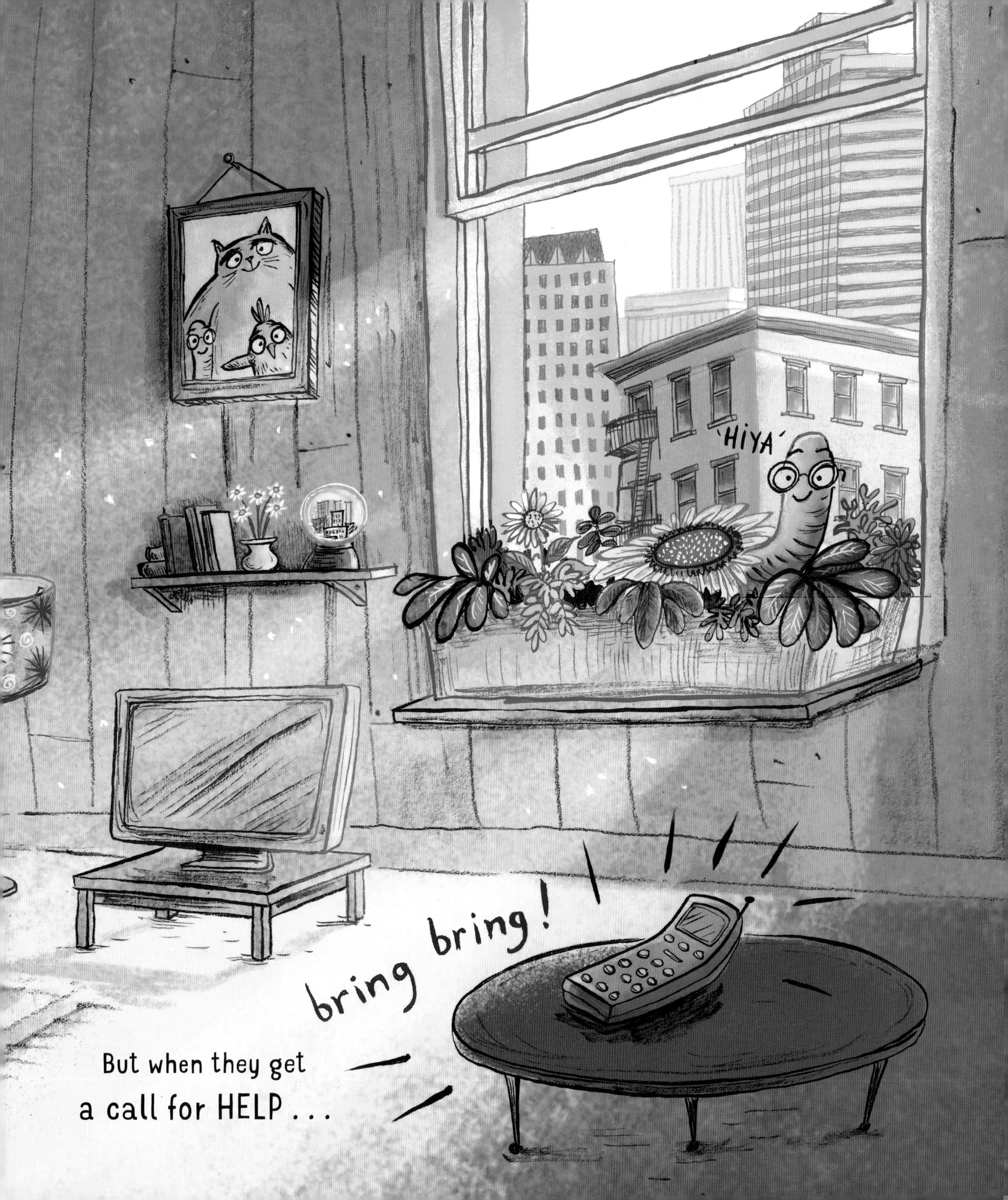
'HIYA'
bring bring!

But when they get
a call for HELP . . .

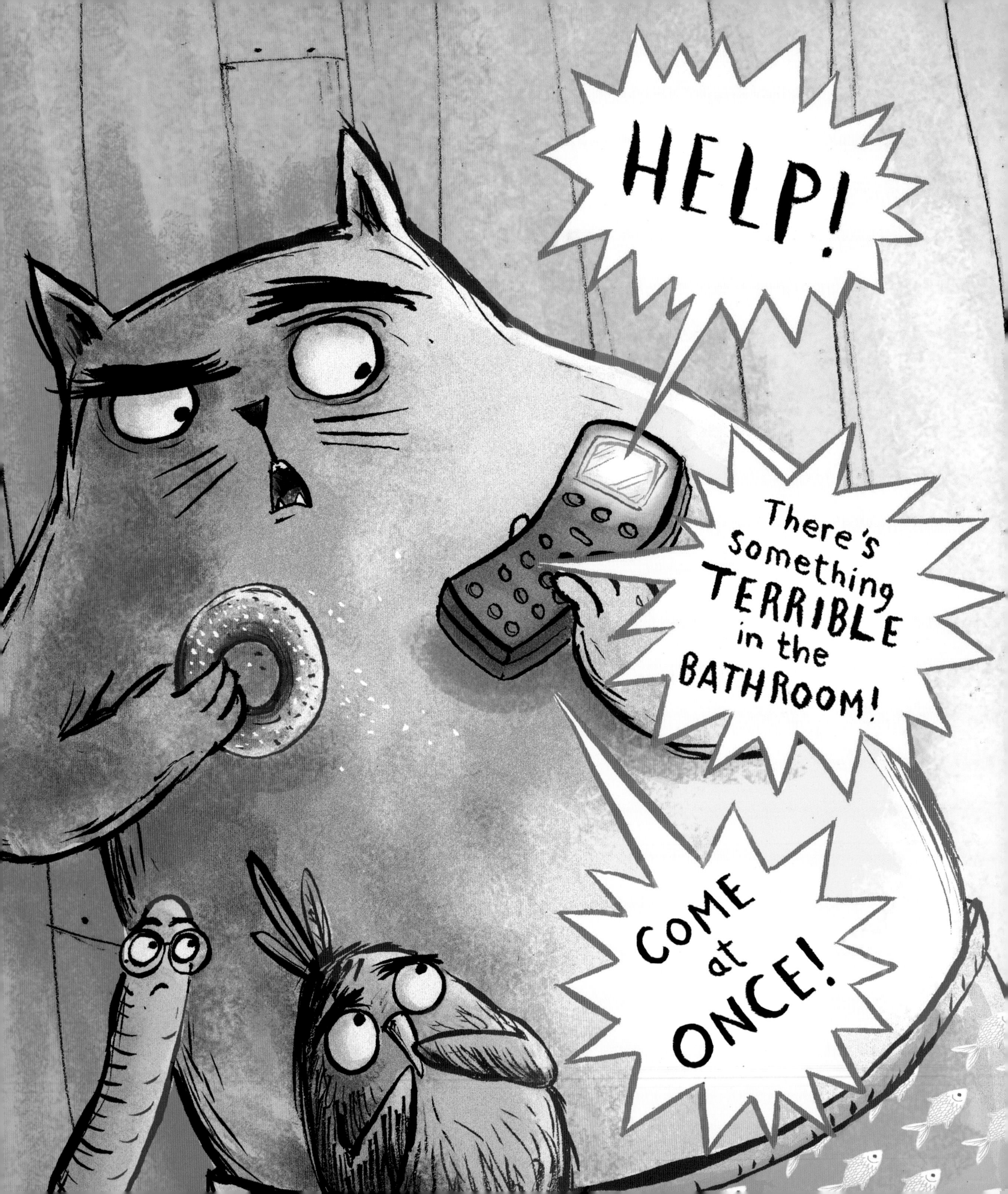
HELP!
There's something TERRIBLE in the BATHROOM!
COME at ONCE!

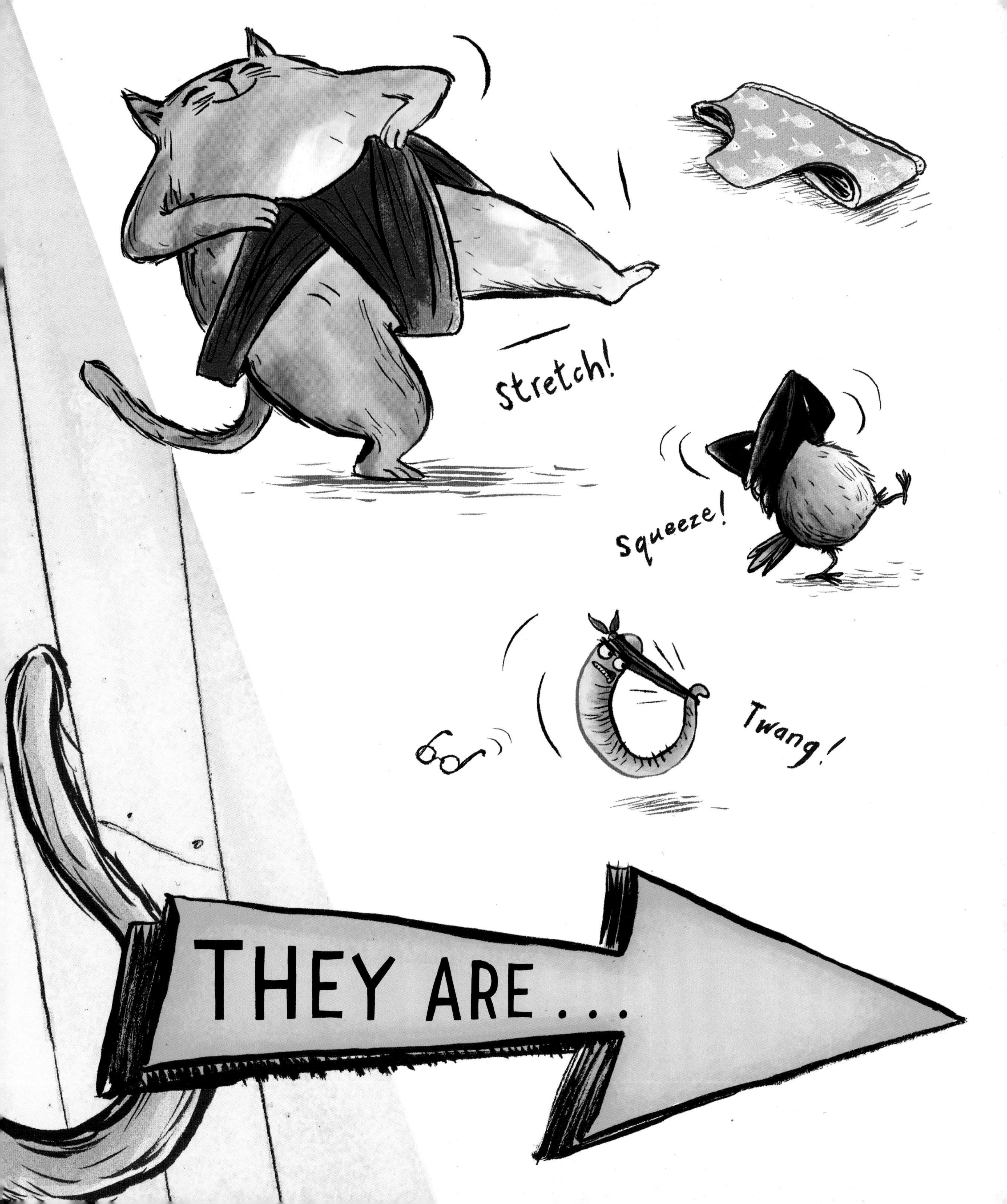
Stretch!
Squeeze!
Twang!
THEY ARE . . .

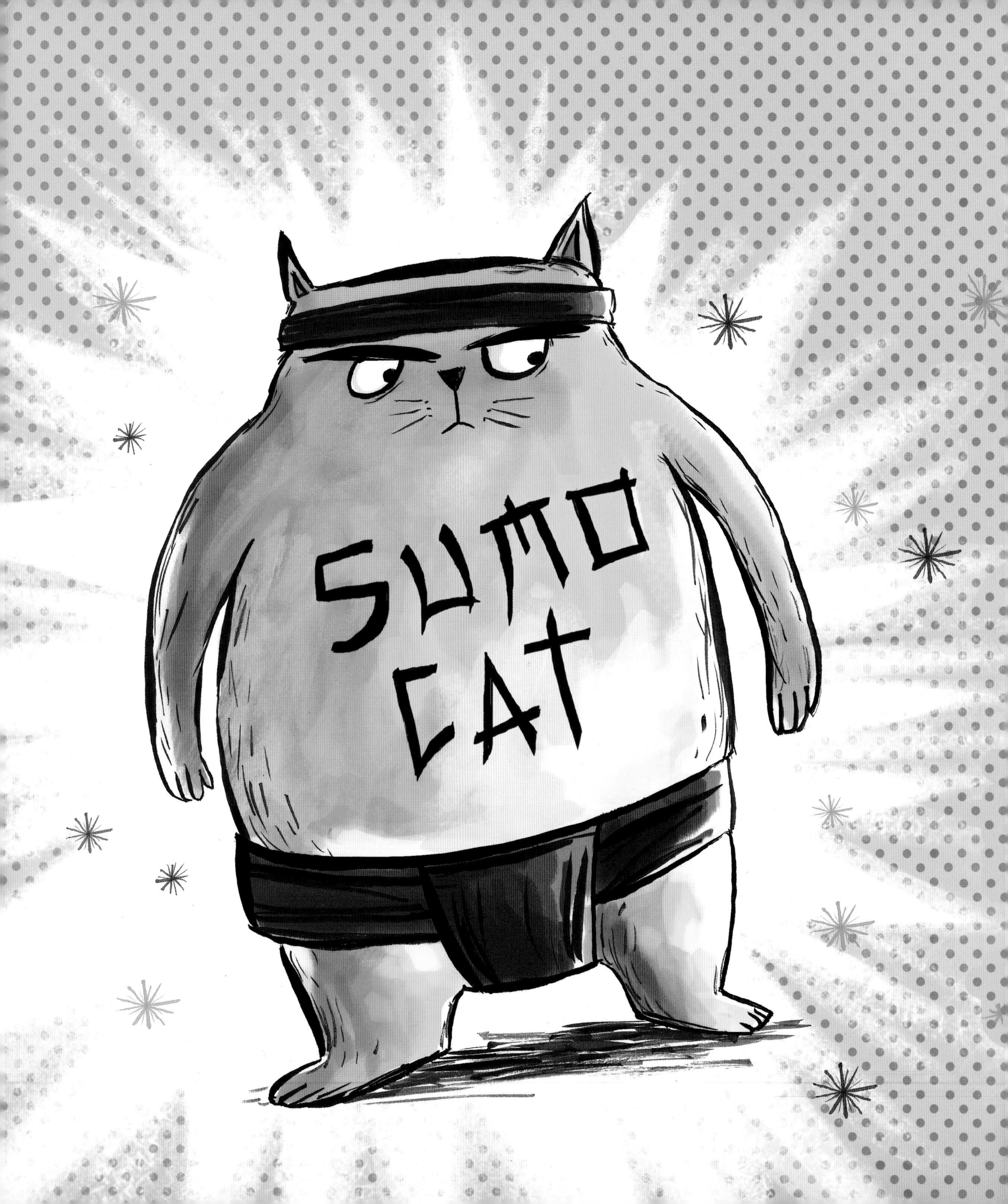
SUMO
CAT

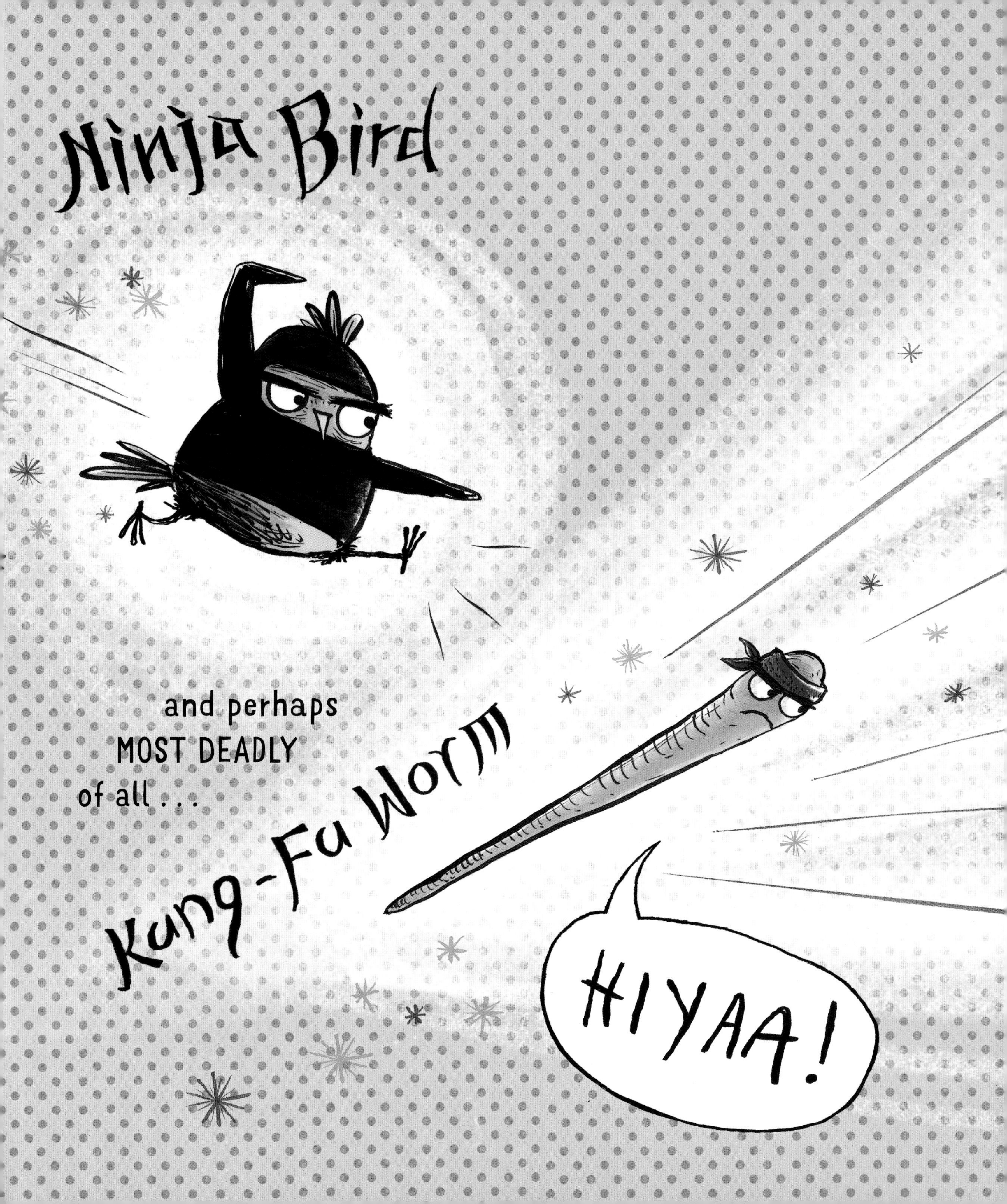
Ninja Bird
Kung-Fu Worm
HIYAA!

and perhaps
MOST DEADLY
of all . . .

"DON'T PANIC!"

cry THE DON'T PANIC GANG

after receiving today's DESPERATE call . . .

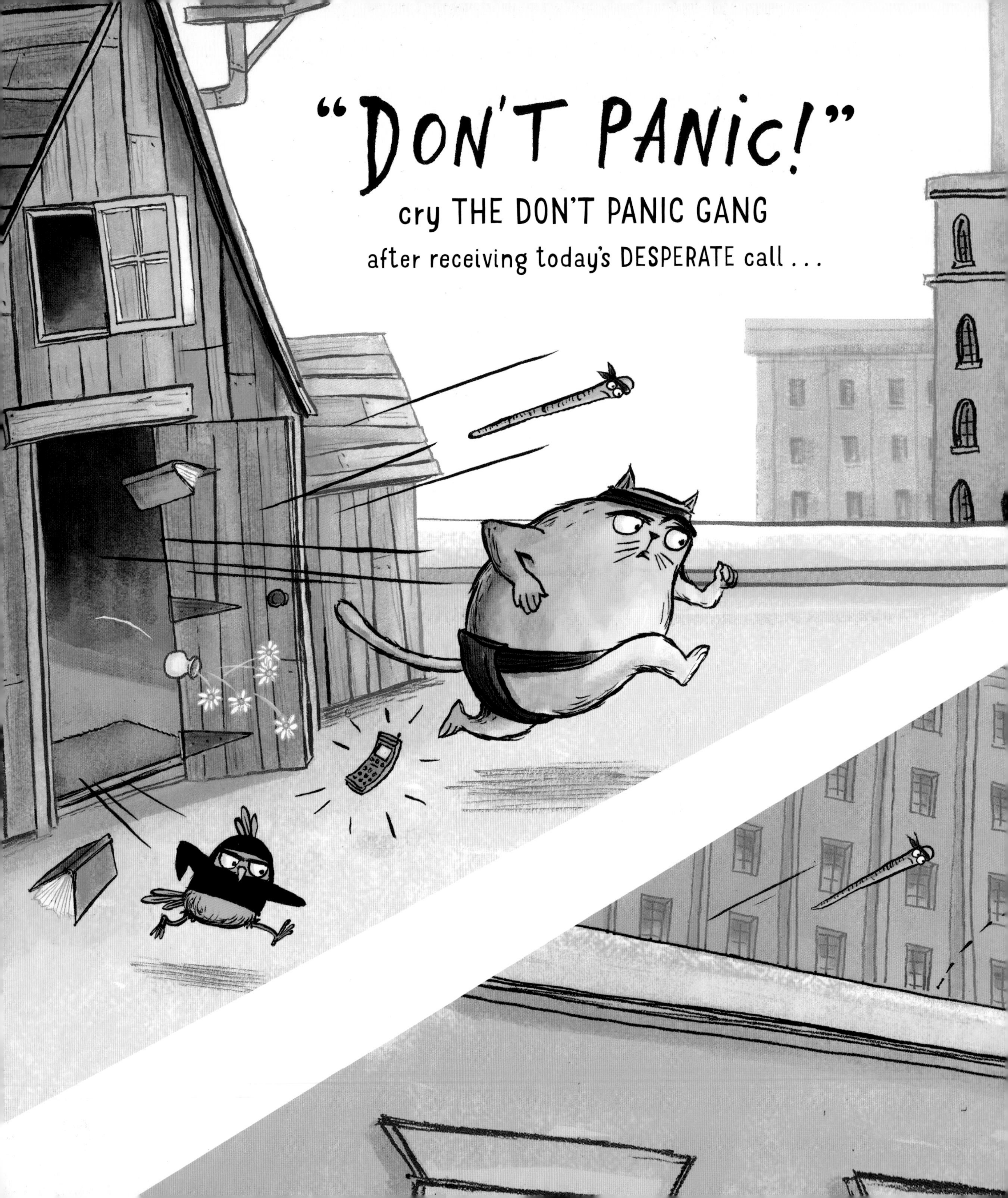

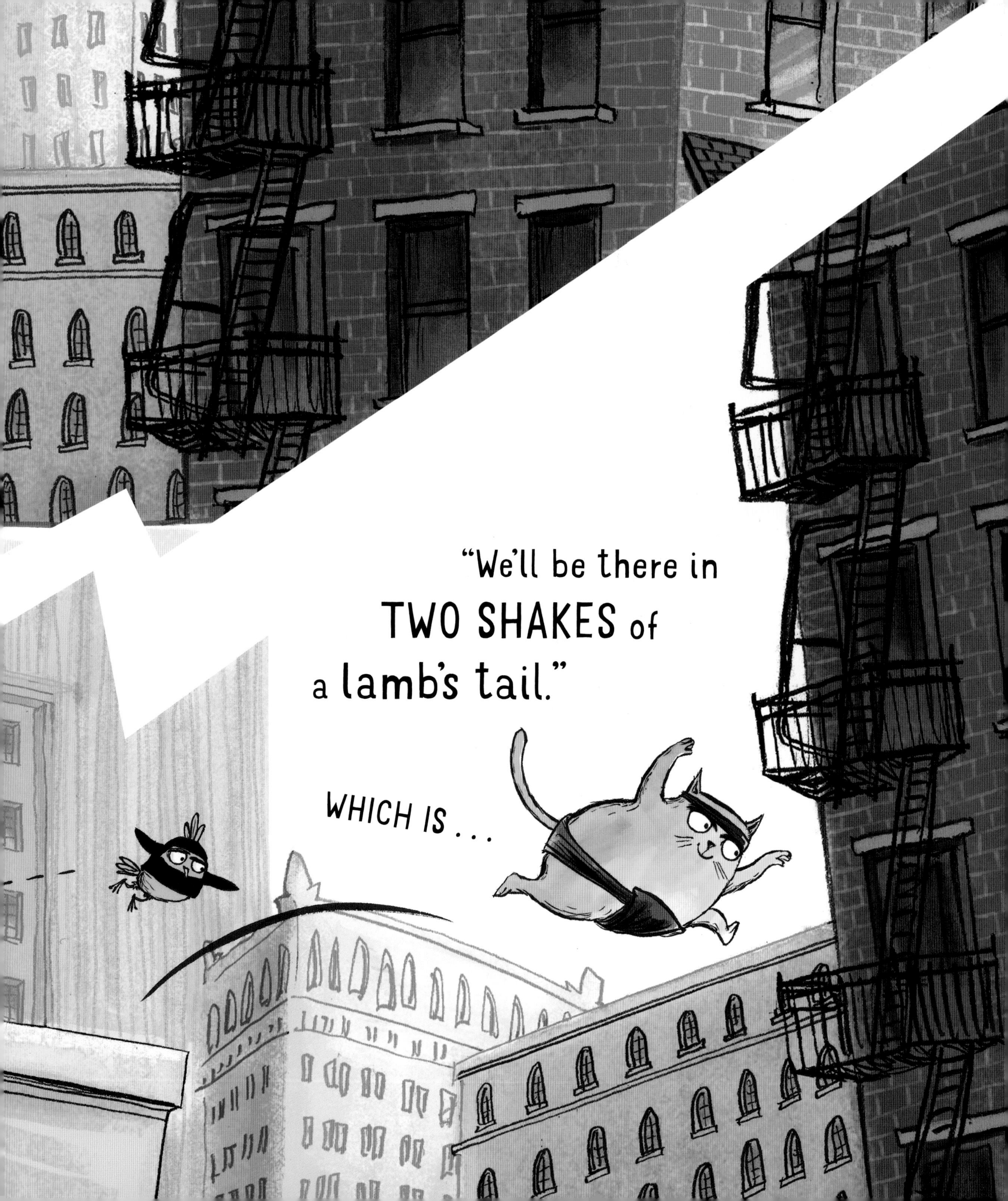

"We'll be there in
TWO SHAKES of
a lamb's tail."

WHICH IS . . .

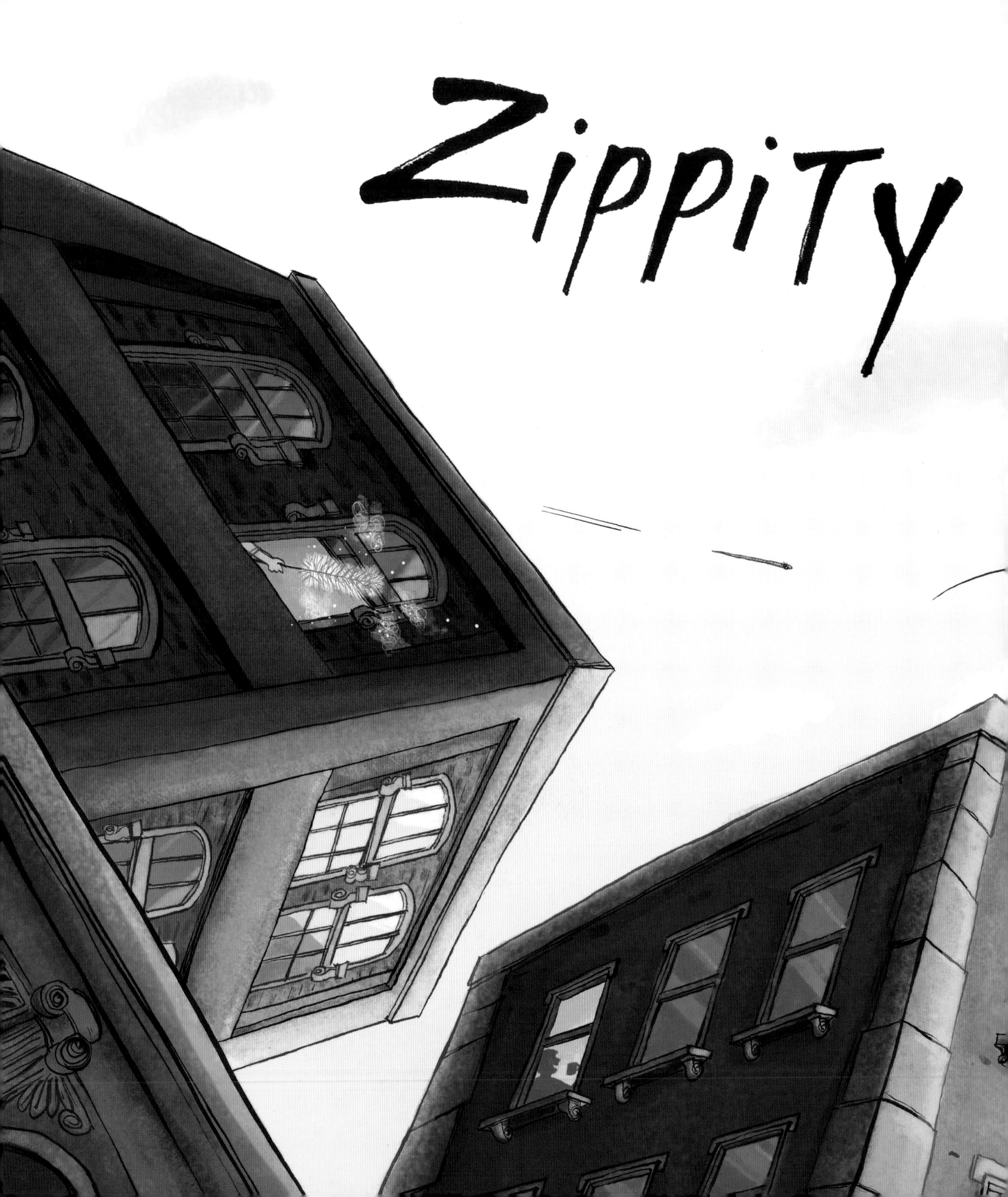
Zippity

Quick!

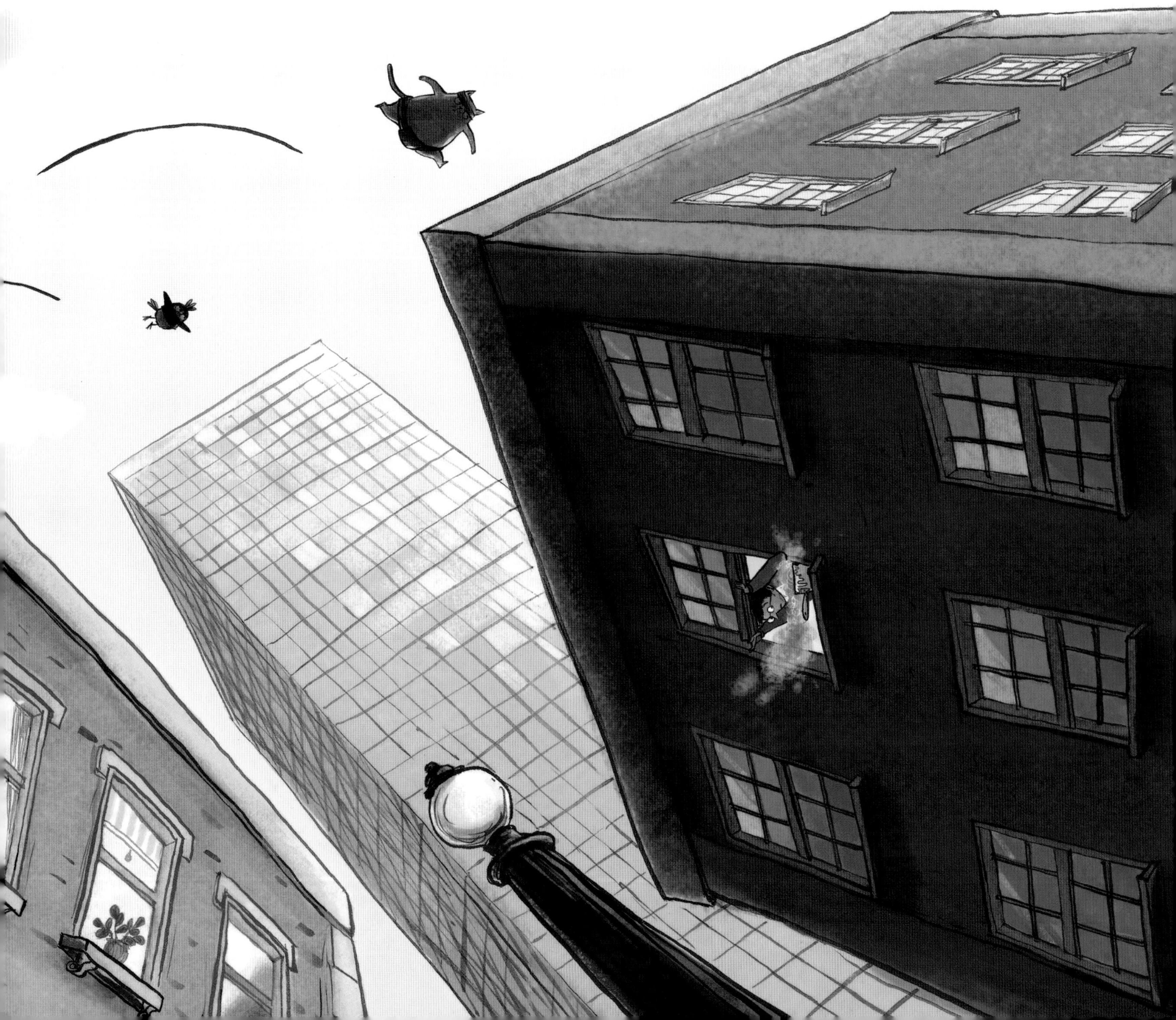

As our three INTREPID heroes CRASH, BUMP and THUD towards the bathroom window, the cries for 'HELP!' grow louder and LOUDER . . .

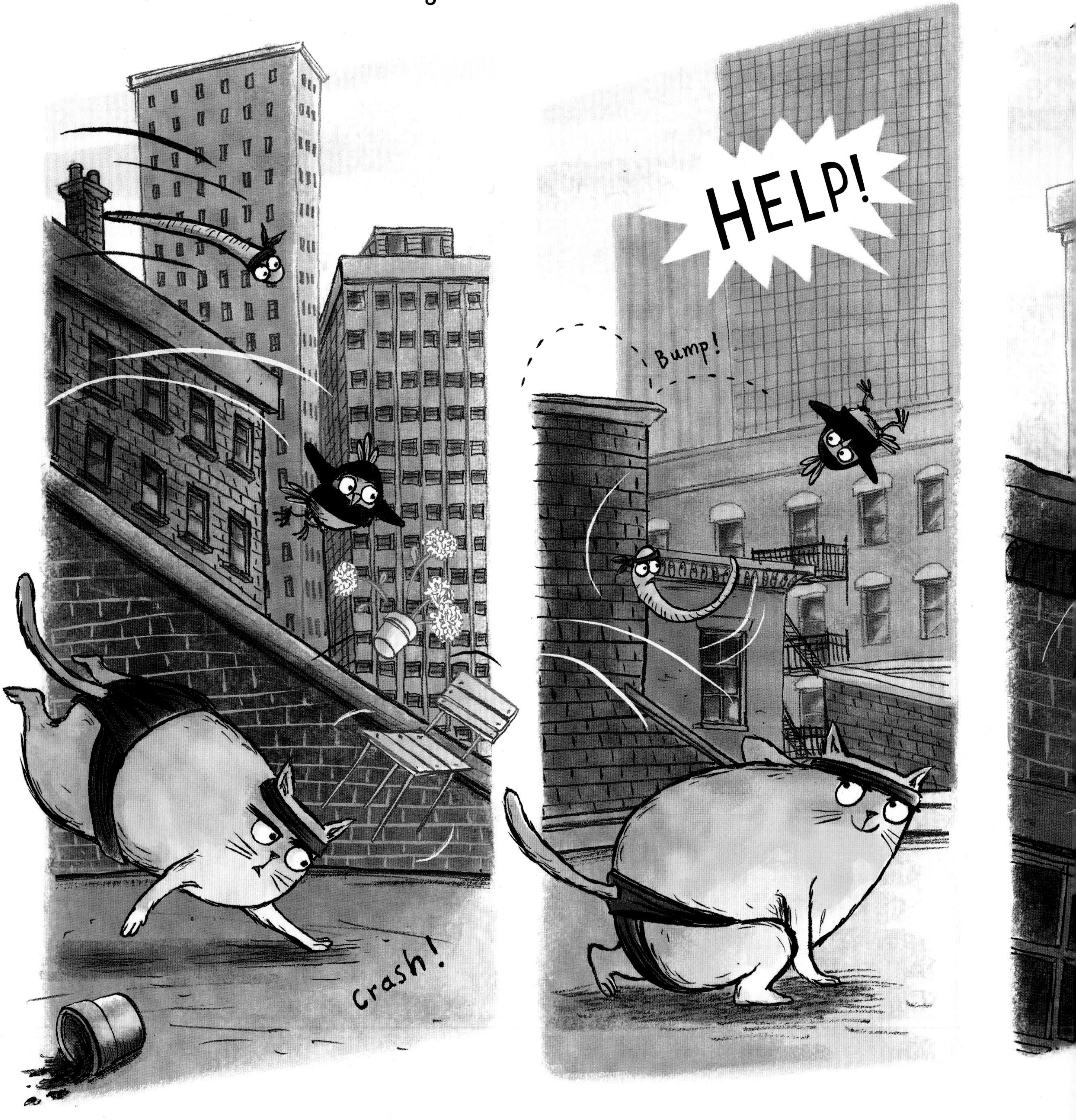
HELP!
Bump!
Crash!

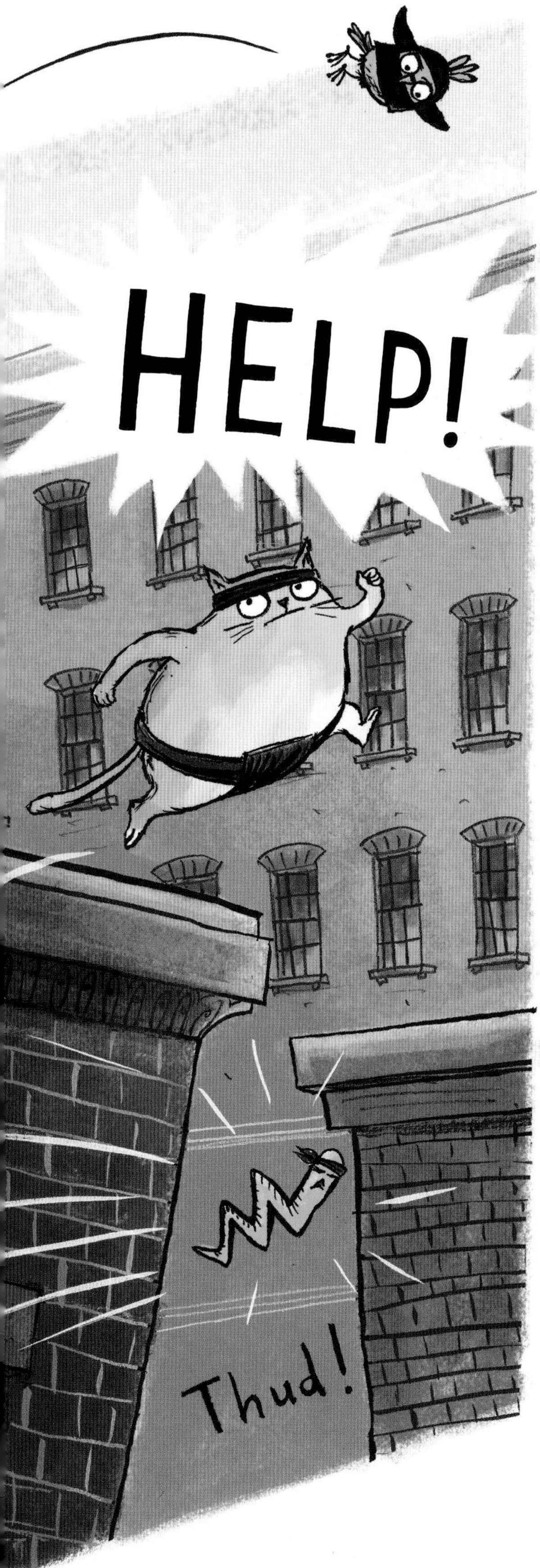
HELP!
Thud!

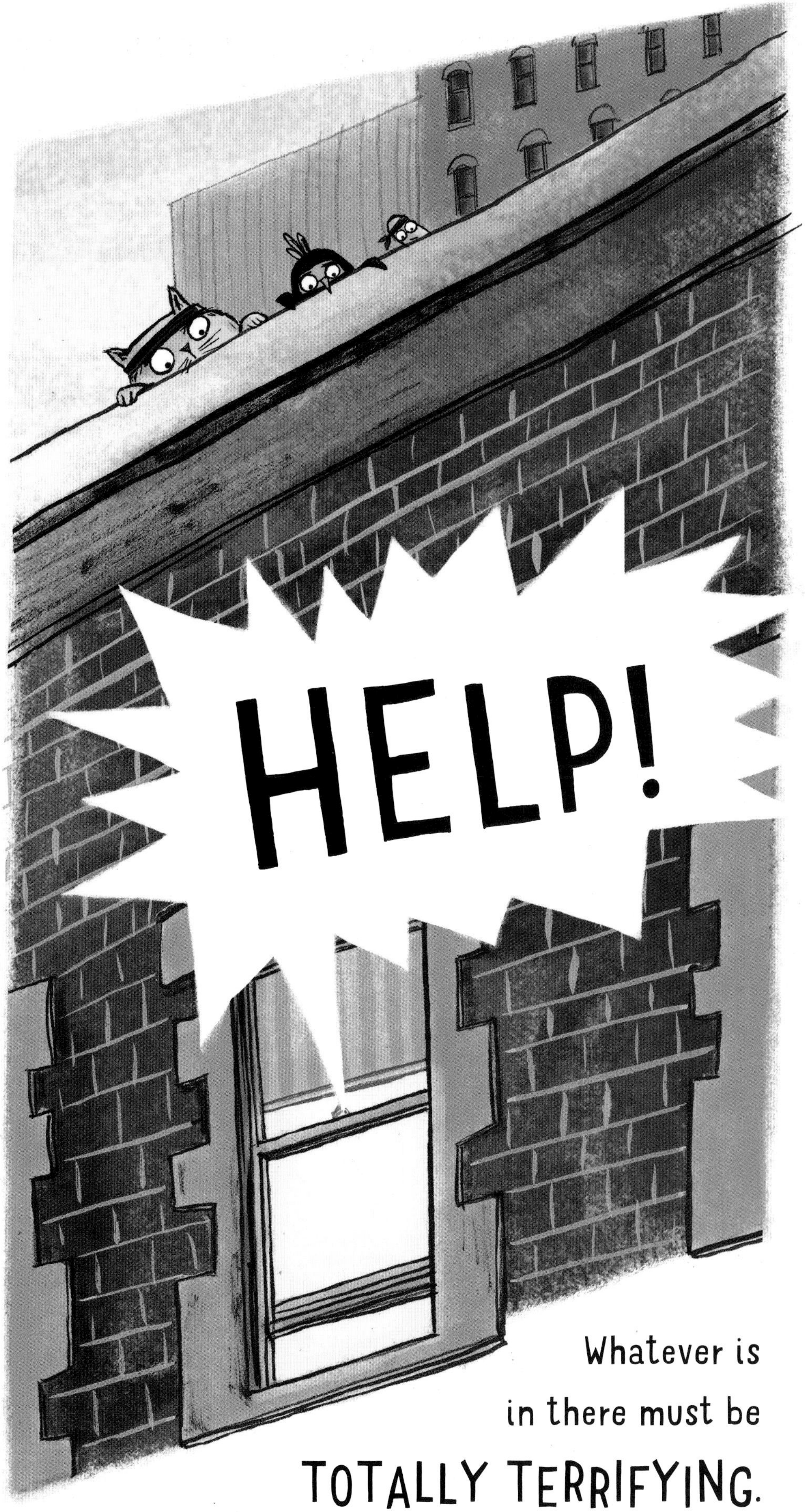
HELP!

Whatever is
in there must be
TOTALLY TERRIFYING.

But Sumo Cat, Ninja Bird and Kung-Fu Worm have **no time** to panic. After all, they are

THE DON'T PANIC GANG

and are

RIGHT HERE to HELP.

So they
fearlessly

and
furlessly

clamber down the wall then peer
through the open window.

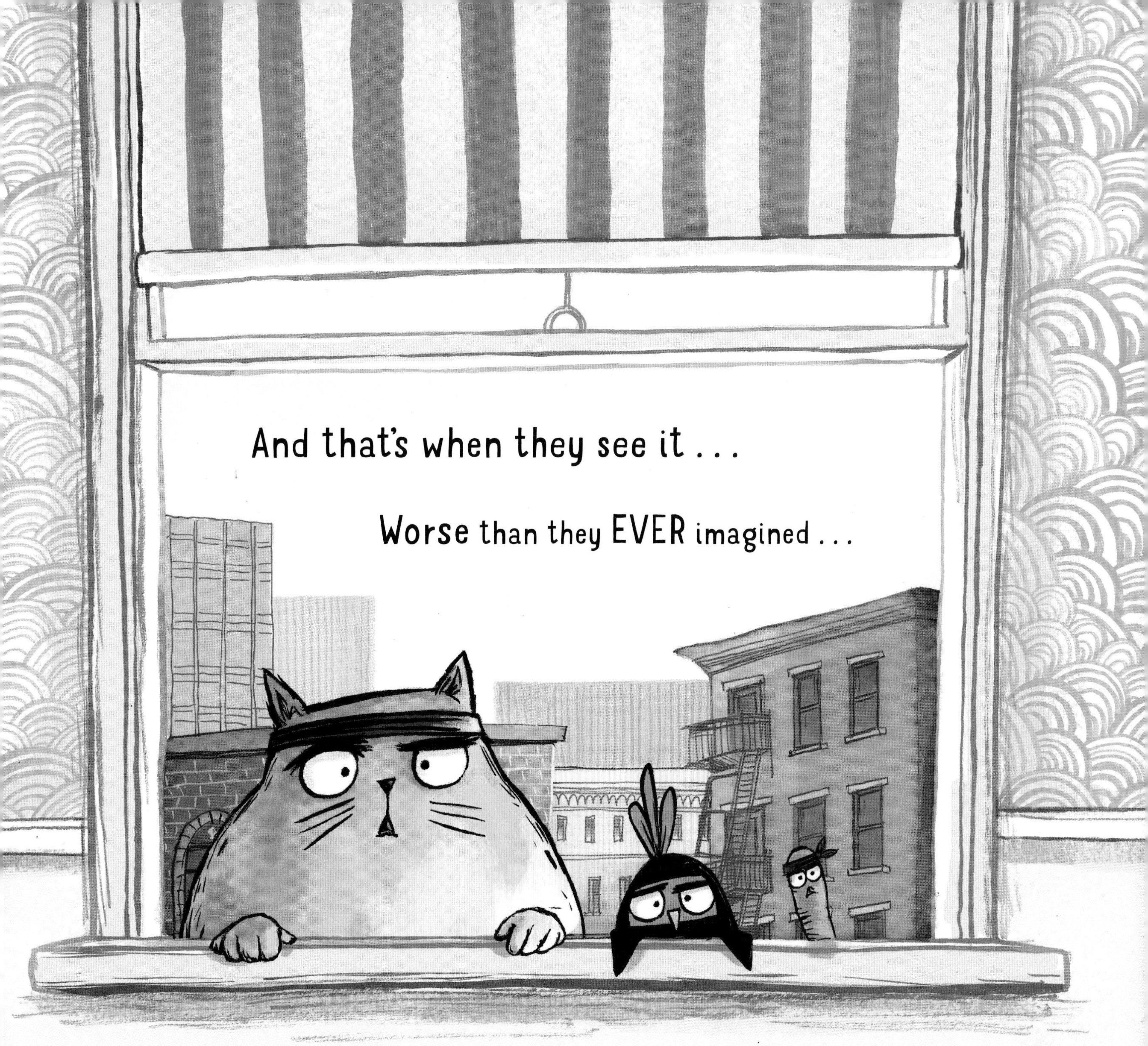

And that's when they see it . . .

Worse than they EVER imagined . . .

Something **HUGE** and **NASTY**

and, yes, TOTALLY TERRIFYING.

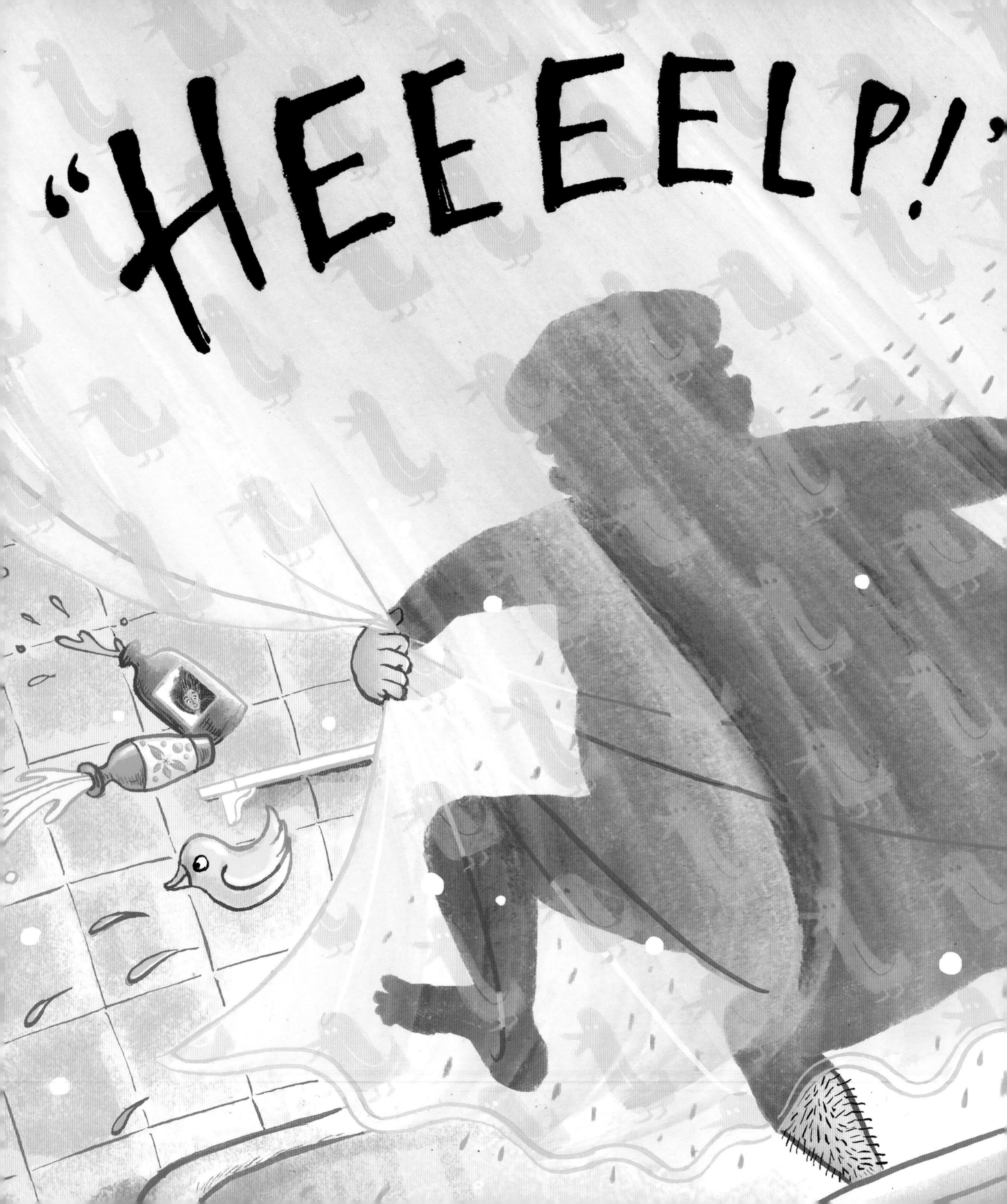
"HEEEELP!"

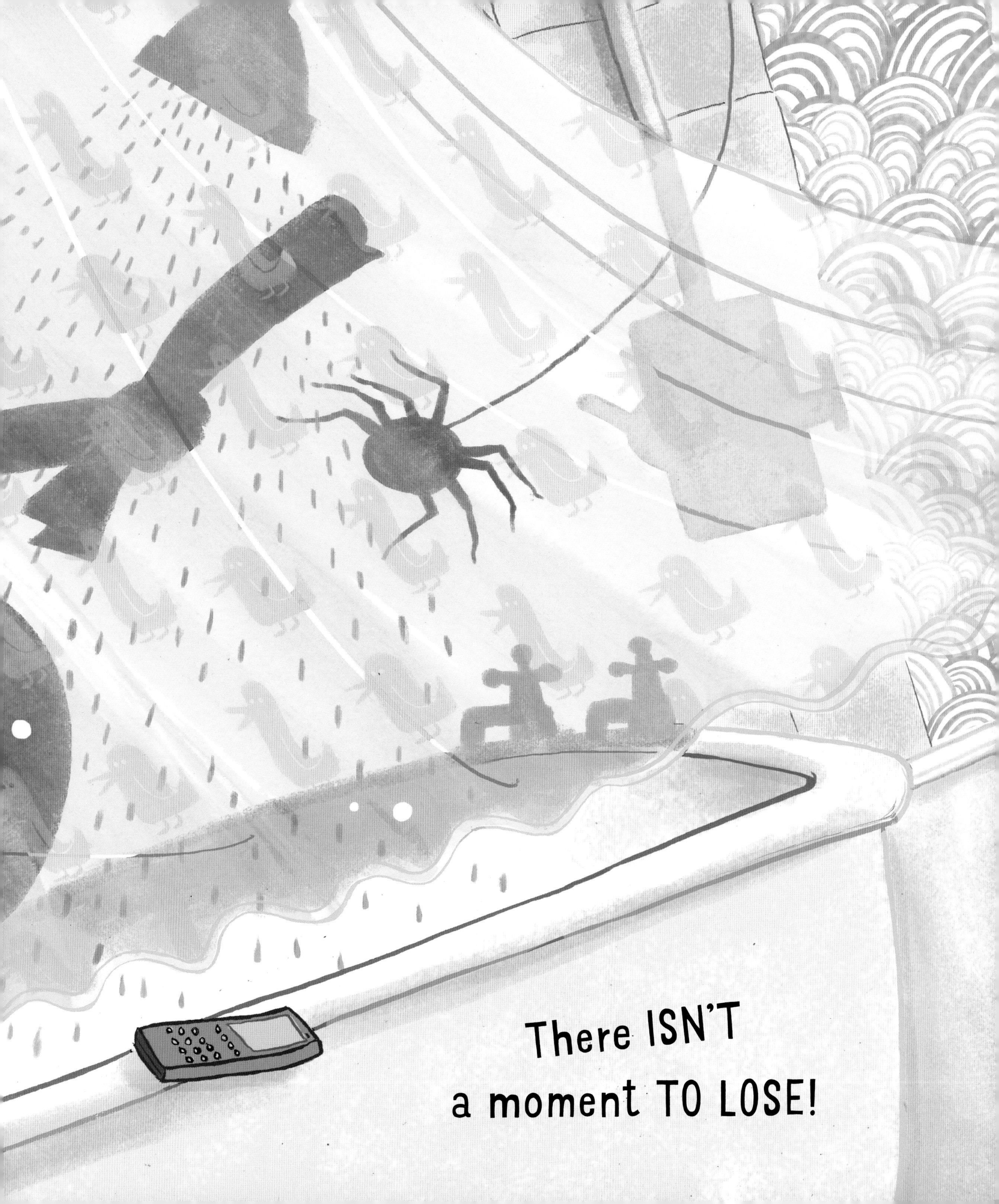

There ISN'T
a moment TO LOSE!

So . . .

QUICKITY ZIP!

with a SUMO stomp

SUMO CAT

sends a blast of

DAZZLING WHITE

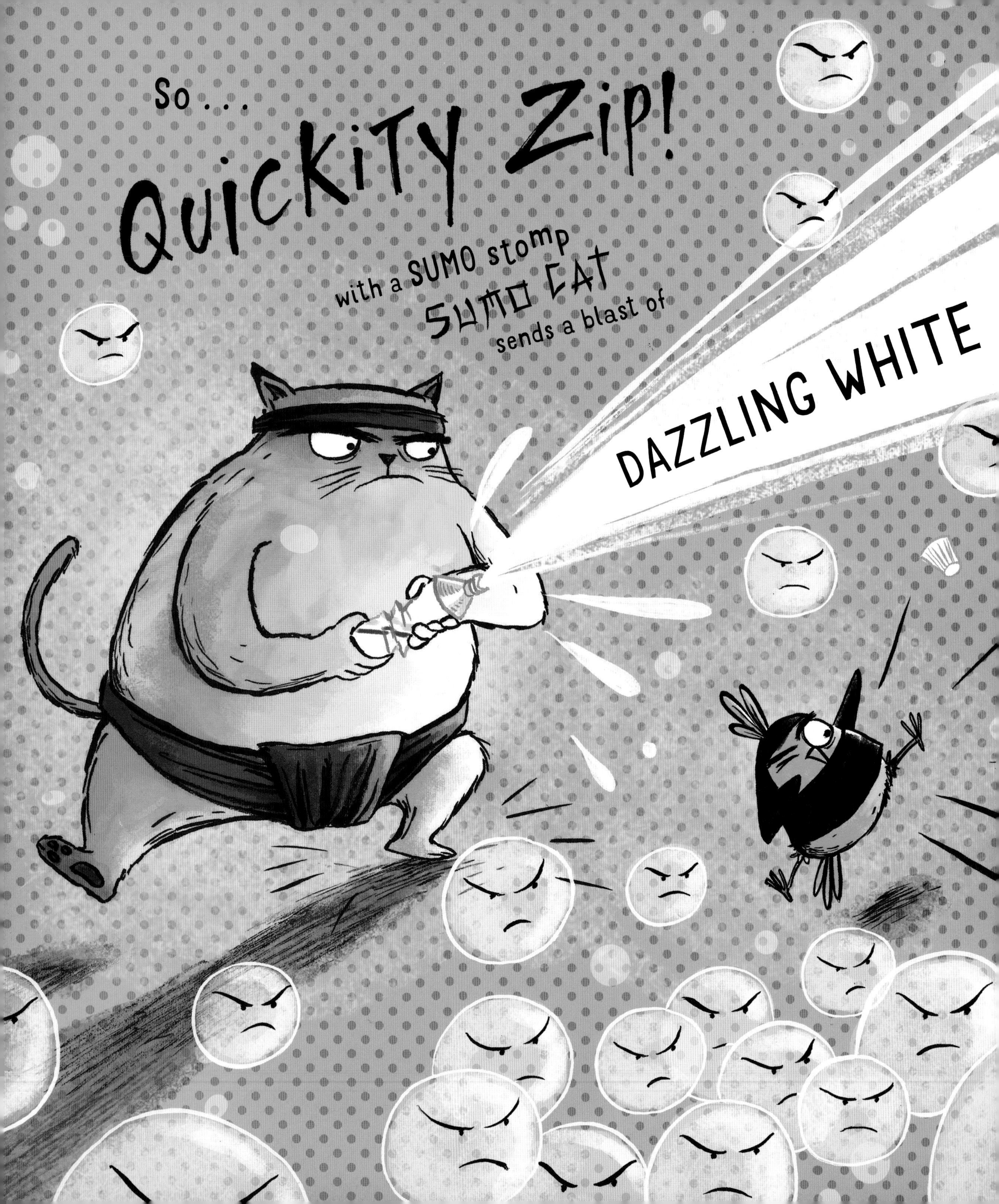

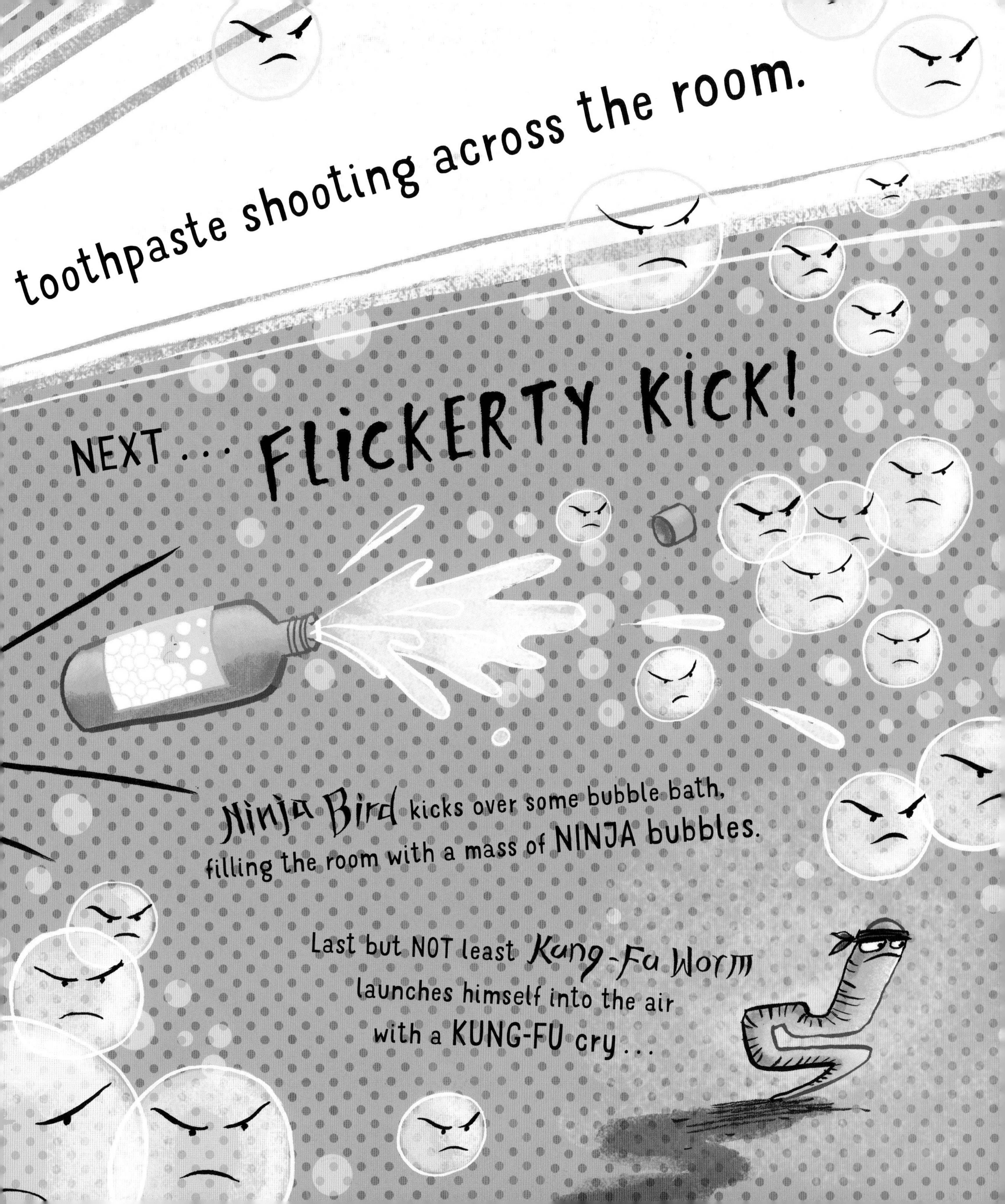

toothpaste shooting across the room.

NEXT . . . FLICKERTY KICK!

Ninja Bird kicks over some bubble bath, filling the room with a mass of NINJA bubbles.

Last but NOT least Kung-Fu Worm launches himself into the air with a KUNG-FU cry . . .

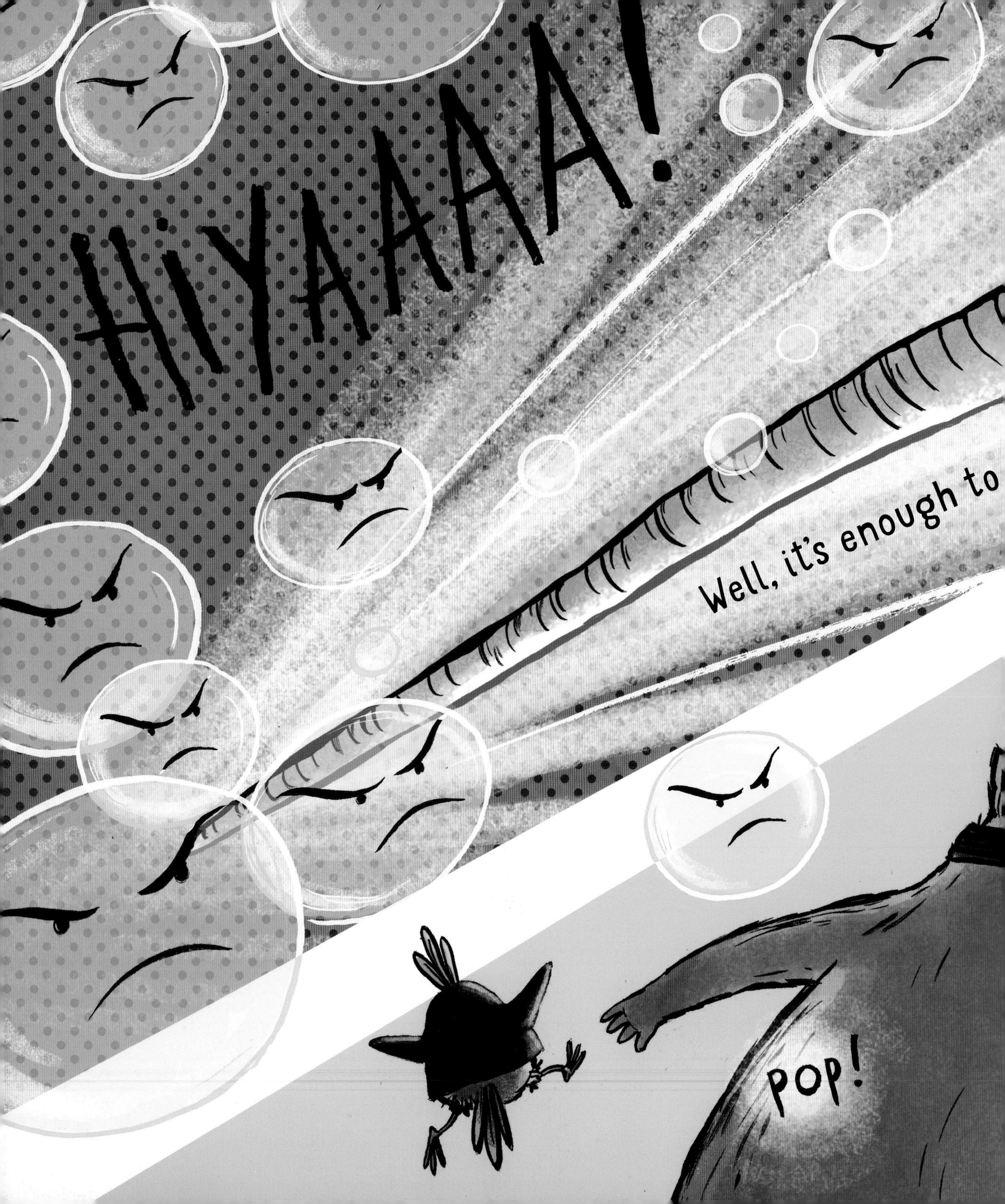
HIYAAAA!
Well, it's enough to
POP!

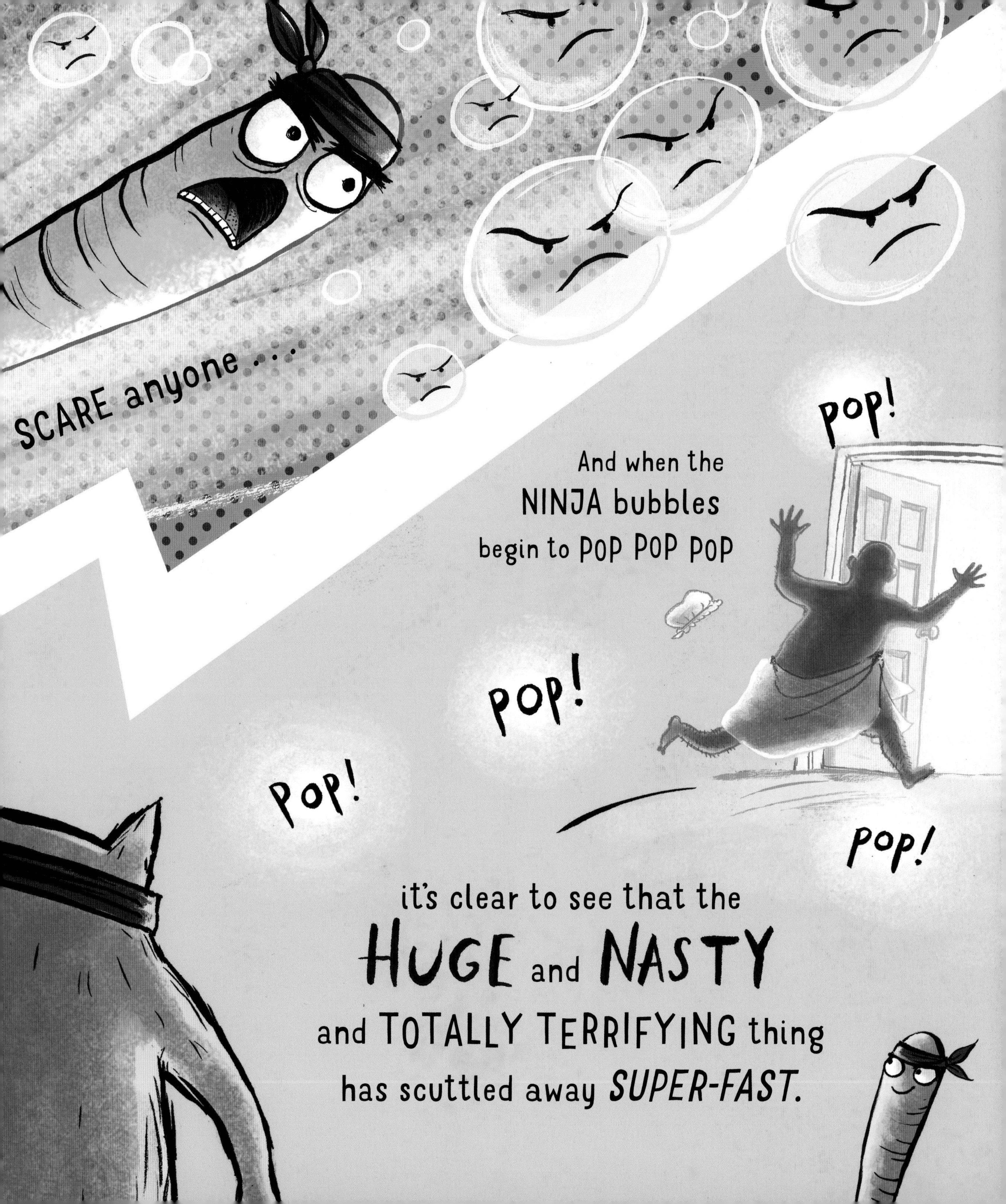
POP!
POP!
POP!
POP!

SCARE anyone . . .

And when the NINJA bubbles begin to POP POP POP

it's clear to see that the **HUGE** and **NASTY** and TOTALLY TERRIFYING thing has scuttled away *SUPER-FAST.*

And all that remains is one VERY grateful little spider.

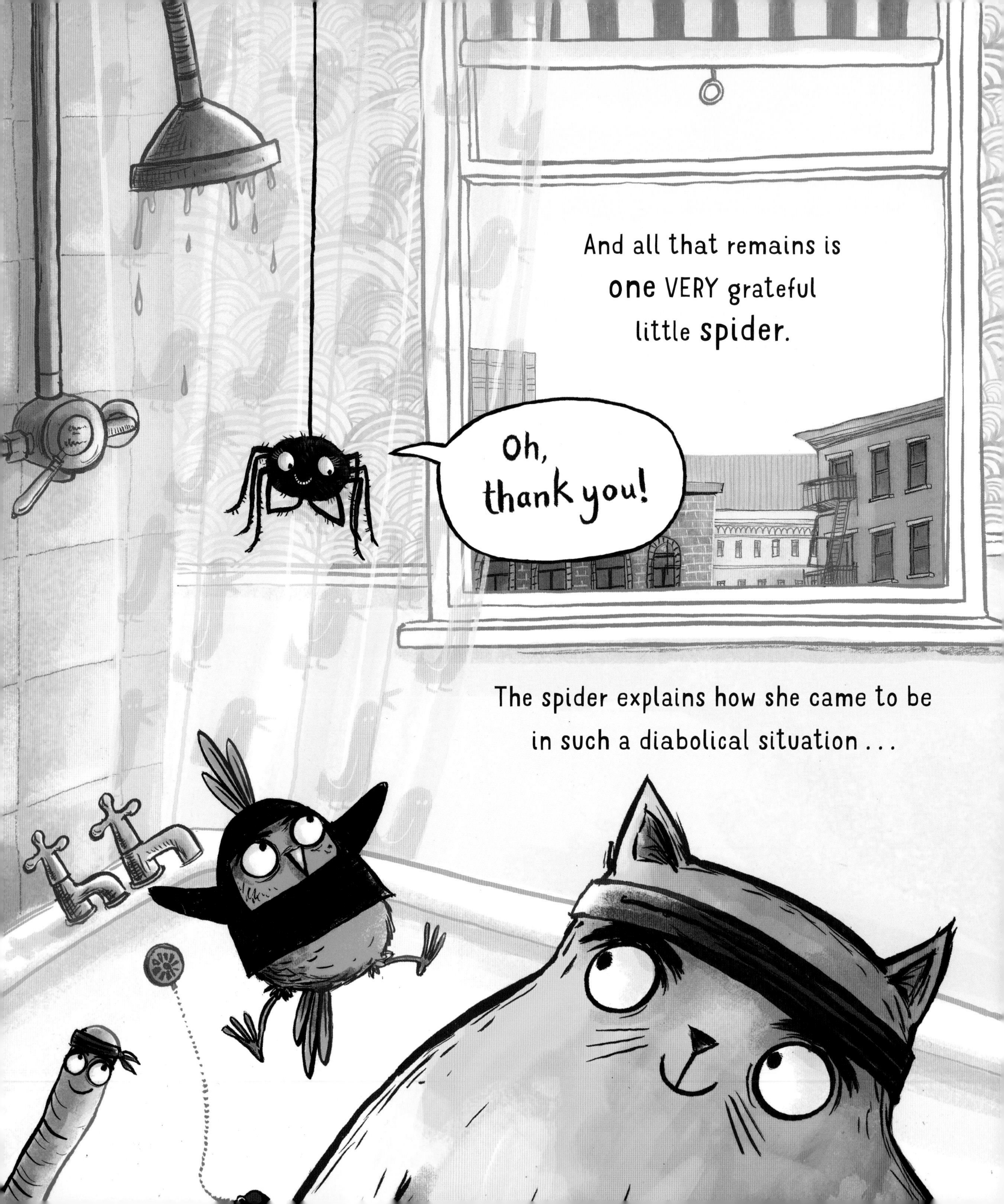
Oh, thank you!

The spider explains how she came to be in such a diabolical situation . . .

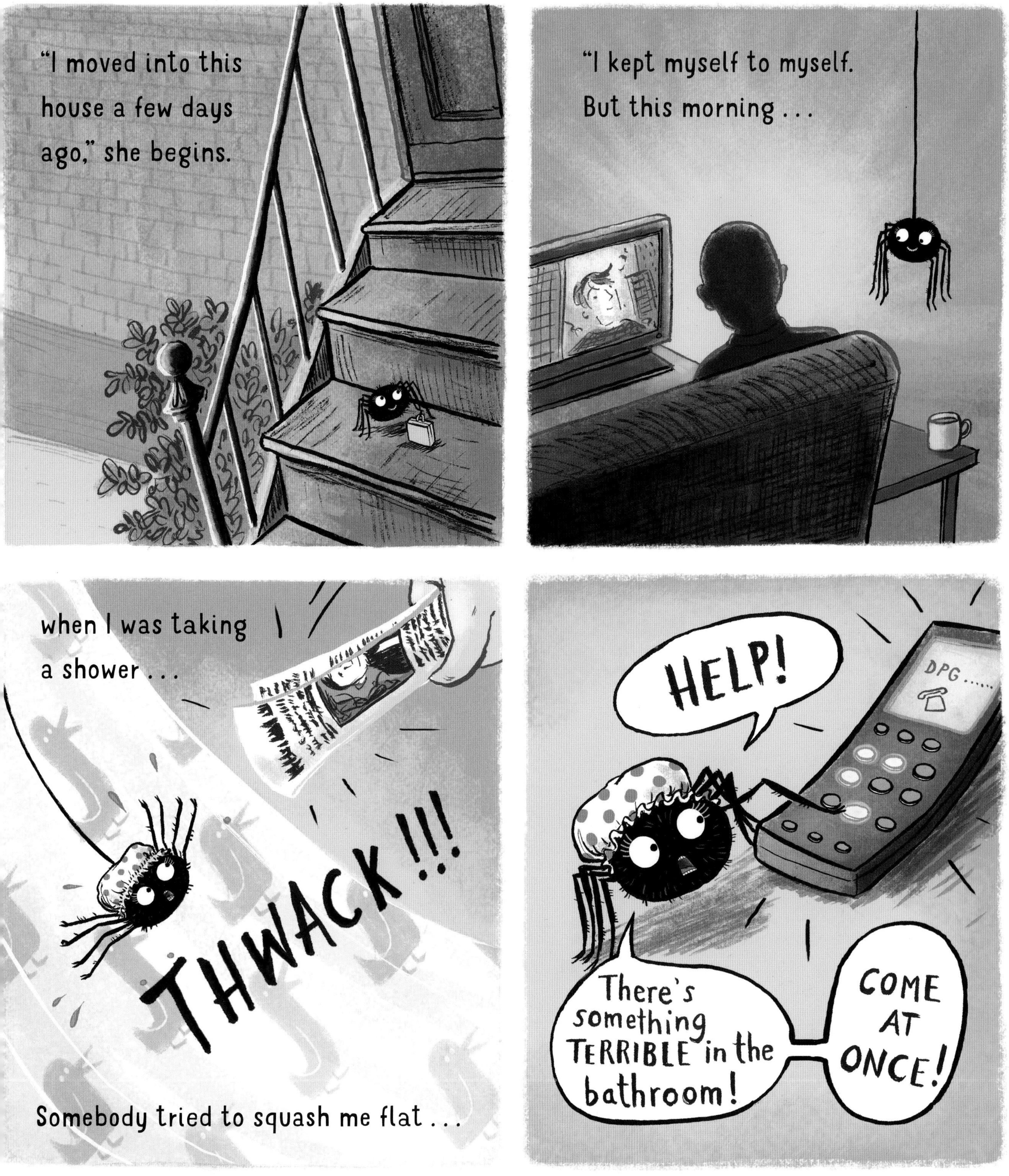
"I moved into this house a few days ago," she begins.
"I kept myself to myself. But this morning . . .
when I was taking a shower . . .
THWACK!!!
Somebody tried to squash me flat . . .
HELP!
DPG......
There's something TERRIBLE in the bathroom!
COME AT ONCE!

THE DON'T PANIC GANG tell the spider they are **so glad** she called. But perhaps it's **BEST** if she comes to **live** with them in their

HOMELY HIDEAWAY.

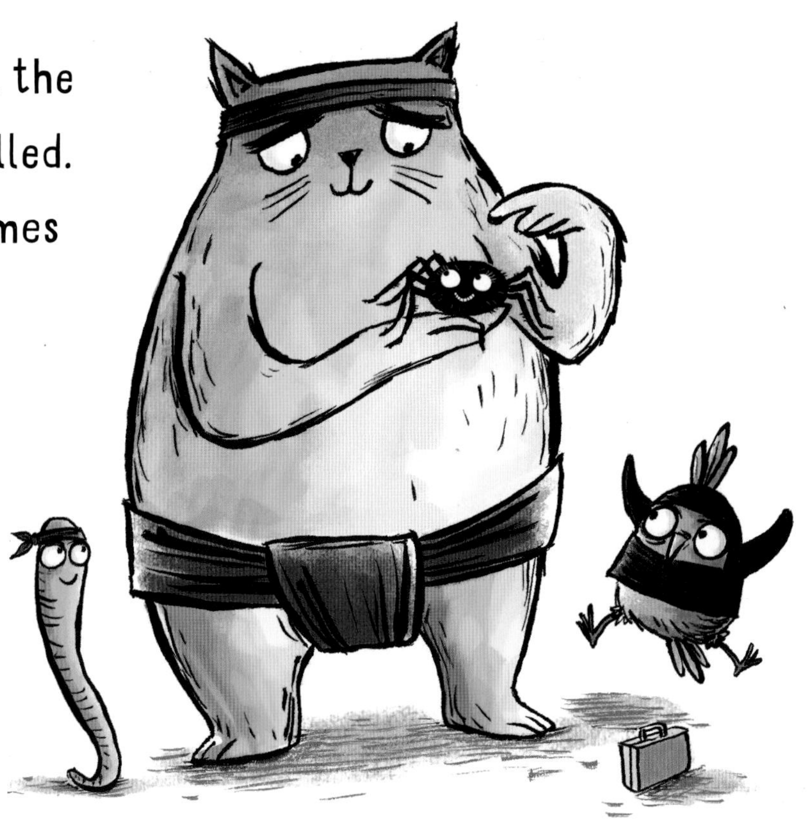

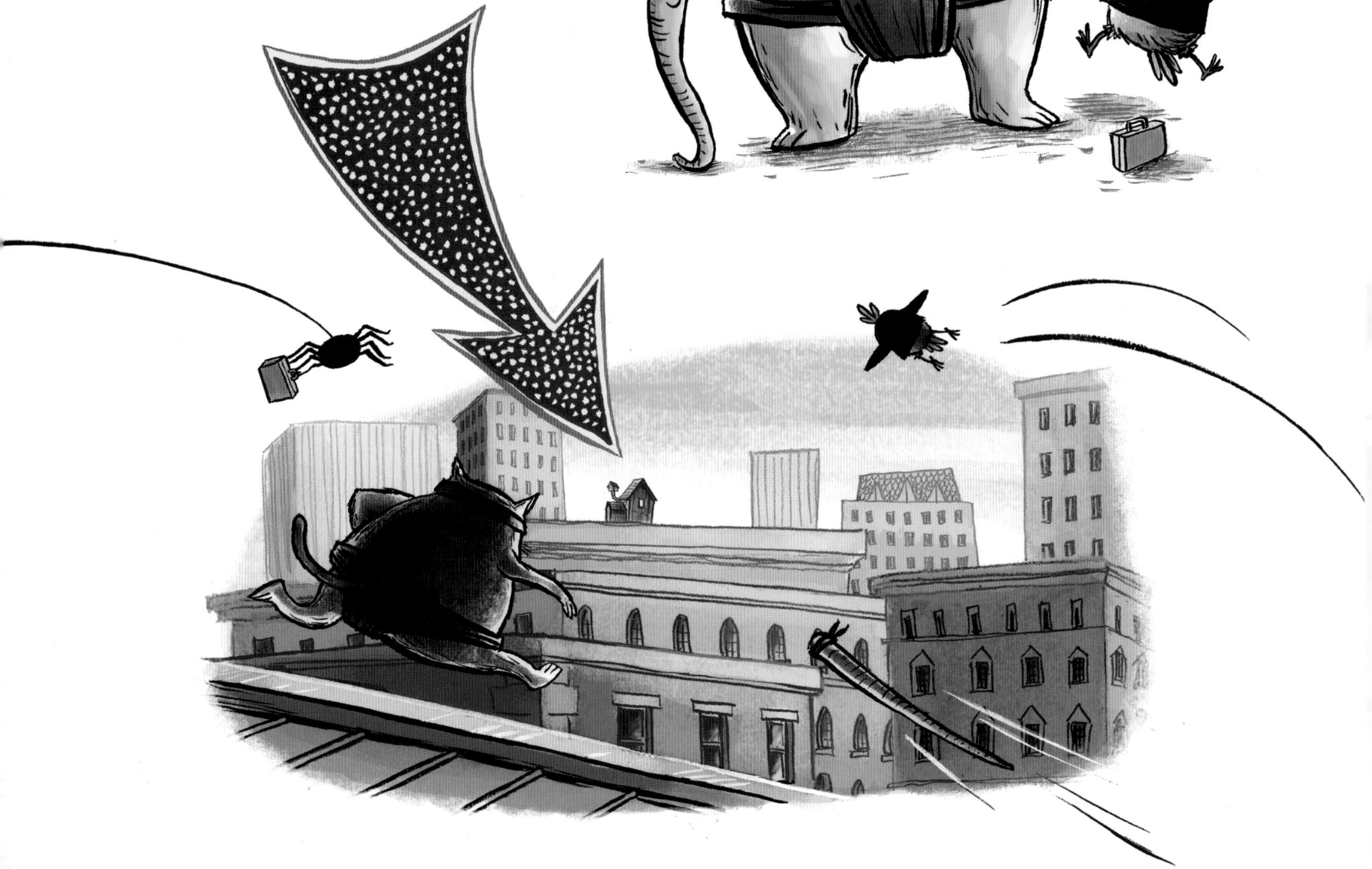

And in **TWO TOOTS** of an **elephant's trunk** (that's *ZIPPITY QUICK*) the whole gang arrive safely back . . .

At their **TOP SECRET** headquarters.

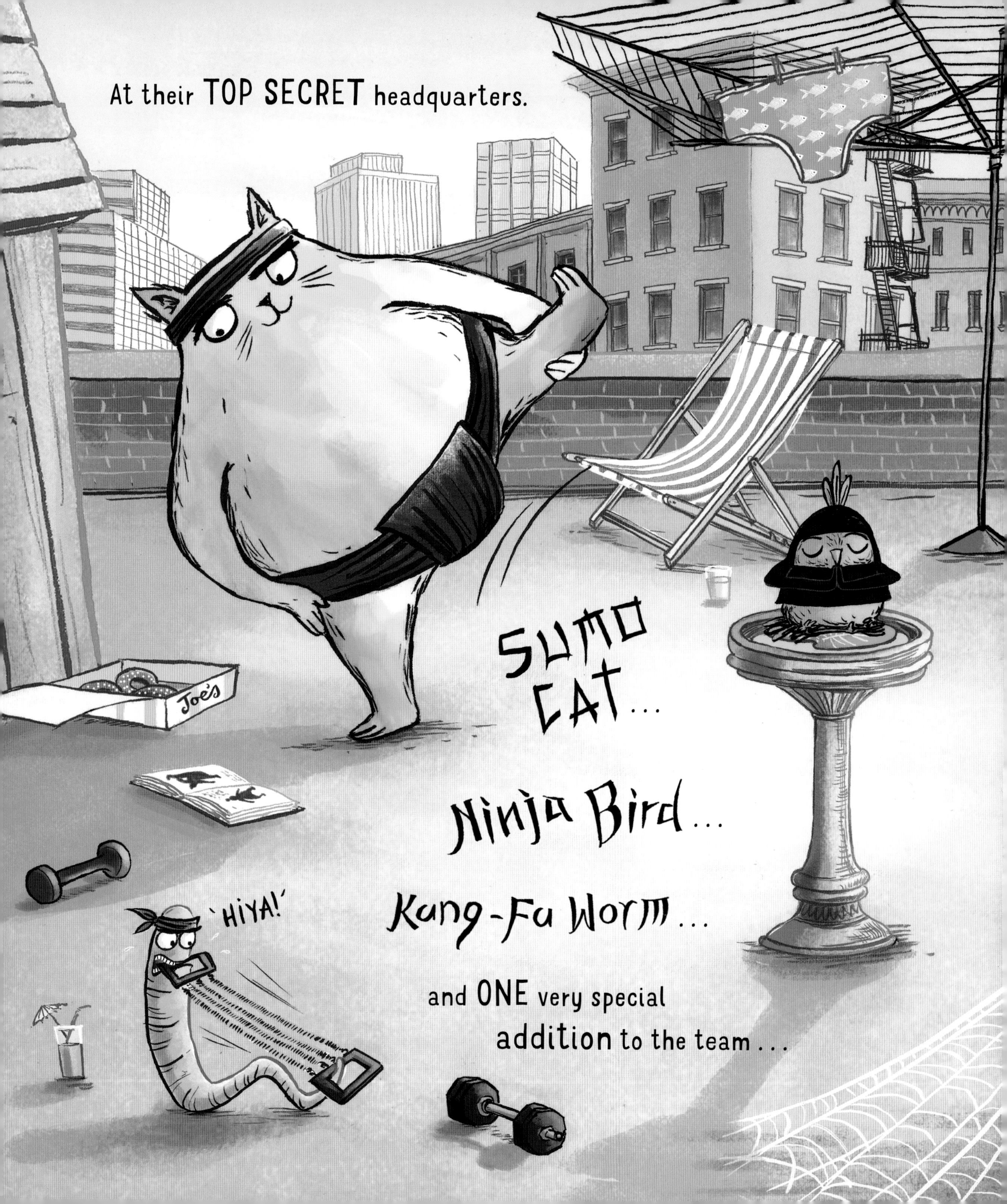
Joe's
'HIYA!'

SUMO CAT...

Ninja Bird...

Kung-Fu Worm...

and **ONE** very special addition to the team...

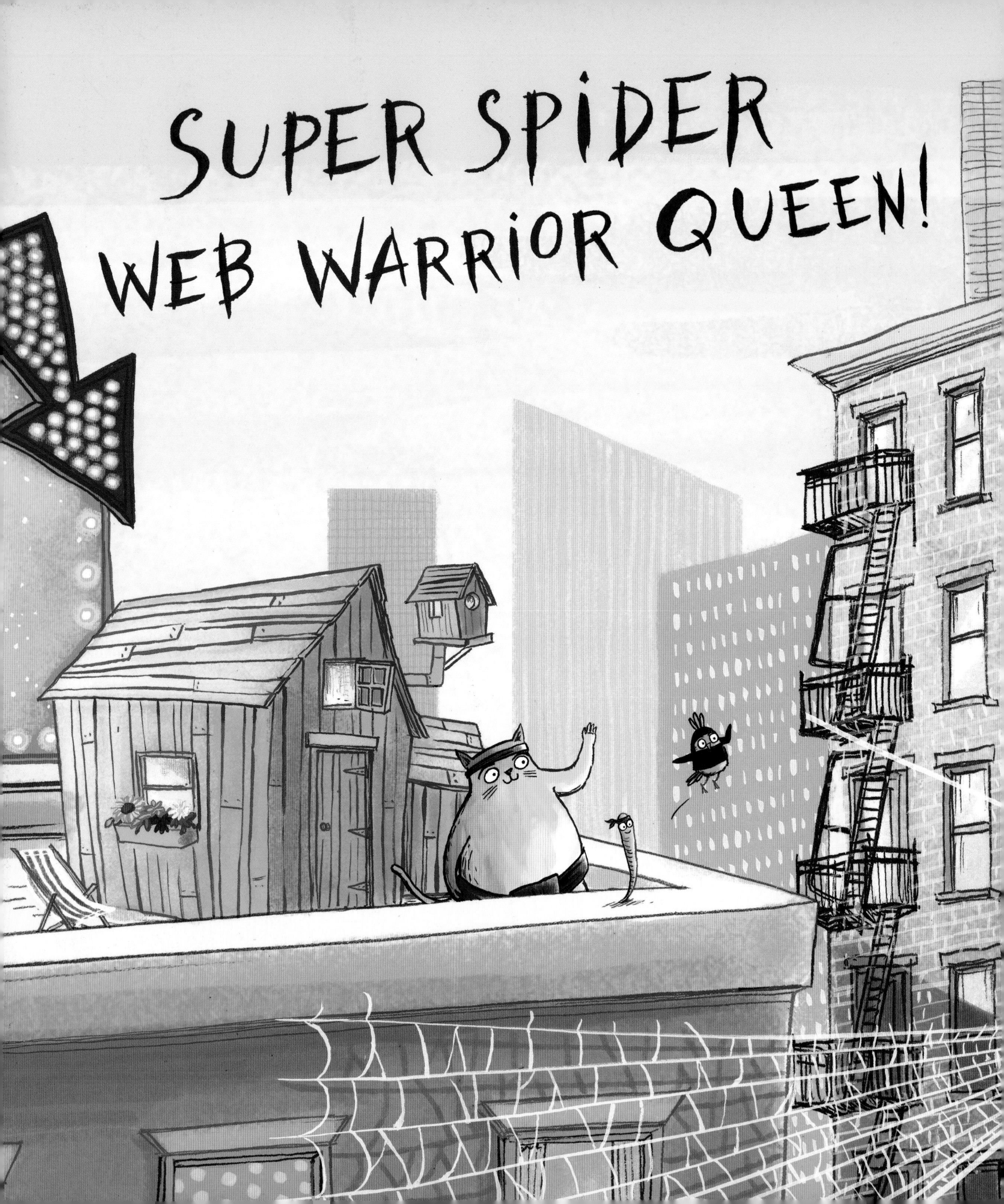
SUPER SPIDER
WEB WARRIOR QUEEN!

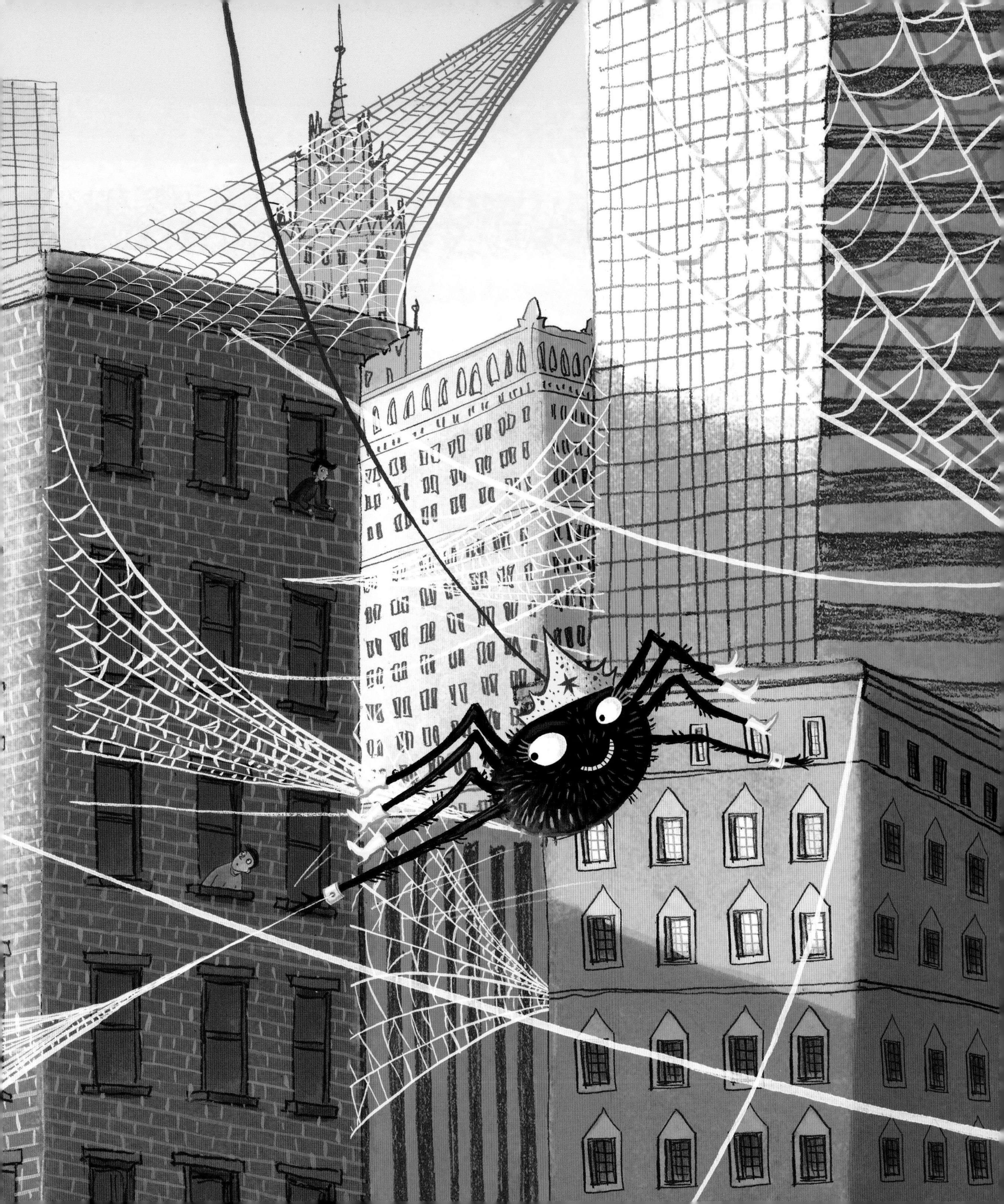

So, just remember if YOU ever need something HUGE and NASTY and yes, TOTALLY TERRIFYING removed from the bathroom...

THE DON'T PANIC GANG
are RIGHT HERE to HELP!

But Shhh don't tell anyone...

'BYE-YAH!'